Breakers

Breakers

N. Brysson Morrison

with an Introduction
by Mary Seenan

Breakers:
Rocks on which waves break; the waves so broken ...
Dictionary

Kennedy & Boyd

Kennedy & Boyd
an imprint of
Zeticula
57 St Vincent Crescent
Glasgow
G3 8NQ
Scotland.

http://www.kennedyandboyd.co.uk
admin@kennedyandboyd.co.uk

First published in 1930
Copyright © Dr. Elizabeth Michie 2009.
Introduction Copyright © Mary Seenan 2009

Cover photograph Copyright © G. Seenan 2009.

ISBN-13 978-1-904999-75 1 Paperback
ISBN-10   1-904999-75 1 Paperback

Introduction

'Och-hey, och-hey,' she was lamenting, 'it's a' bad thegither
that is happening. But ho! It will a' come back on them that causes
it. If ye do bad things, they'll turn on ye in the end like crushies
gone savage.'

- Breakers

Nancy Brysson Morrison's first novel, *Breakers*, was originally
published in 1930, when the author was twenty-six years old.
Born in Glasgow in 1903, she was the fifth child in a family of
six. She was educated at Park School in Glasgow, before spending
a year, 1919-1920, at Harvington College – formerly known as
Heidelberg College – in London. She spent most of her life in
Scotland, living at various locations in the Glasgow area, as well
as at Kilmacolm and Edinburgh, before finally moving to London,
where she died in 1986. Between 1930 and 1974 she produced
ten novels, five biographies, three books with religious themes, and
various short stories and articles. In addition, between 1939 and
1959, she also wrote romantic pot-boilers under the pseudonym
'Christine Strathern'. Some of these were serialised in D.C.
Thomson magazines such as *The People's Friend* and *The People's
Journal,* and twenty seven of them were published by Collins.

Breakers, however, shows no romantic tendencies. Set in the
early years of the nineteenth century, it is a dark novel which follows
the fortunes of three generations of the family of the minister of
a poor parish situated at the edge of a Highland loch. Readers
familiar with Morrison's later novel, *The Gowk Storm* will recognise
the setting of the Barnfingal manse and the isolation it imposes,
particularly on the female members of the family.[1] Like *The Gowk
Storm*, this novel also has a subtext which has wider ramifications
than the surface narrative would seem, at first reading, to suggest.[2]
But the thematic concerns of *Breakers* are very different. For, while
the surface narrative has an intimate focus as it follows the fortunes
of Callum Lamont, the minister's unacknowledged, illegitimate
grandson, as he tries to take by force the birthright he has been

denied, the subtext widens its scope to question representations of Scottish literary, social and economic history that had, until then, remained largely unchallenged.

That Morrison intended her novel to convey a deeper significance than that of a simple story set in a bygone age, is suggested by the title and the definition of the word 'breakers' which prefaces the text: 'Rocks on which waves break; the waves so broken...'. This definition, delivered before any action takes place, emphasises the importance of the shifts in perspective offered within the novel. It stresses, too, the indeterminate nature of language, and, particularly in the ellipsis, it opens up the possibility of a multiplicity of meanings. This is particularly significant in the prioritisation of the different types of ideologically-inscribed discourse of which the novel is composed, for this is one important area in which *Breakers* challenges conventional expectations. In addition, the definition's conflation of cause and effect undermines the principle of causality on which historical theories have been based. Most importantly, in this respect, it suggests that the Enlightenment concept of linear historical progress, from barbarism to civilisation, reflected and endorsed by earlier historical fiction, such as that of Scott, can be replaced by a cyclical, repetitive view of history. Finally, the connotations of violence and destruction, with which the definition is imbued, provide a menacing undertow for the book as a whole.

As a first novel, *Breakers* is not without flaws. Perhaps foremost among these is the apparent mis-match between the opening section, dealing with the middle-class manse family, and the subsequent action which, somewhat abruptly, leaves them behind to focus on the unwanted grandson. However, while it is true that this opening section is rather long in terms of its importance in plot development, it does highlight the Gillespies' character flaws and ideological preoccupations, so that they provide a contrast to the more humble concerns of ordinary country folk explored in the rest of the book. Such a fault should, I think, be forgiven in the light of the novel's two major strengths. These are its introduction of the Clearances from the perspective of the dispossessed Highlanders, and its exploration, in its portrayal of Callum and Fiona, of those elements of Scottish experience and sensibility, previously found in Hogg and Stevenson, which continue to disturb and disrupt the nation's idea of itself and its past.[3]

The pivotal historical event in *Breakers* is the brutal eviction of the inhabitants of Inchbuigh farm and their neighbours on the Marquis of Moreneck's estate to make way for the more lucrative rental income from large sheep farms, grouse moors and deer parks. The Highland Clearances, as they are now understood, had not, until then, appeared in Scottish historical fiction. One earlier, very different, account of how the population of a glen had been removed is found in Annie S. Swan's novel *Sheila*.[4] However, in that portrayal there is no obvious intention to disrupt what was then the generally-accepted Establishment view that the Clearances were simply a means of agricultural improvement and vital for the nation's economic progress. Nor is there any intention to question the financial probity of the landed gentry. In fact, the book is prefaced by a poem dedicated to the Duchess-Dowager of Athole, whose family owned Glen Quaich where the action is set.

In *Sheila*, the villagers leave the Fauld clachan of their own volition, to escape the mercenary machinations of the factor, who, it is stressed, originally belonged to their own class. Furthermore, they are shown to benefit from the experience by finding greater health, wealth and happiness soon after what has apparently been an envigorating voyage to Canada. This is a far cry from the unsentimental delineation of the hardships of Highland life and the descriptions of roof burning, crop destruction, and eviction of sick and dying tenants offered in *Breakers*. It differs, too, from Morrison's description of the aftermath of the Inchbuigh evictions:

> For more than a week spiral columns of smoke could be seen coming from the charred ruins of the cottages. By that time the uncertain ghosts who had peopled the moors after the evictions had all been driven away. Many went to Canada in a ship so rotten they could pick the wood out of her sides with their fingers. Some died of smallpox and dysentery on the voyage and the survivors counted them fortunate, for they escaped by death the misery, the poverty and incredible hardship they had to endure. The young men filtered to the Lowlands, where they became weavers or

worked in factories and were thought droll and stupid with their slow, gentle, country manners. But most of the families wandered to the sea shore. They drifted there in hordes until they blackened the narrow, stony beach. [5]

Although from her personal knowledge of what happened on the Breadalbane estates Morrison was aware that, in some instances, population reduction was achieved by the process of attrition – as happens with the Gow farm in *Breakers* – she chose to emphasise the barbarity of many others by fictionalising accounts such as those found in Alexander Mackenzie's *A History of the Highland Clearances*.[6] This intention is made even more obvious by references to the district of Naver and 'whit happened in Sutherland and whit's happening in Ross-shire noo'.[7]

Sympathy for the Highlanders' plight is also engendered in the moving description of the deputation's journey to Gel Castle to plead with the Marquis. Their innate dignity and comradeship is registered in the way in which, 'clad in their Sabbath blacks', their initially hesitant progress 'through the stricken clachans' becomes more courageous as folk join their ranks. Their procession is shown to assume the military bearing for which the Highlander had become renowned:

> Hearts beat quicker, blood rose higher, and the tramp of their feet became almost rhythmic, like the tramp of soldiers. Through the Pass of Naver, over the Fionn moors, ferried across Loch Tarrol, through Drura and Auchendee, past a shabby little manse on the loch's side, to little Barnfingal. Then leaving the Loch, up a steep brae: now through Muccoth and over the wild, turfy hills.[8]

But the martial tempo disappears when they learn that the Marquis has gone to London, and Morrison registers that their failure to halt the evictions sounds the death knell for the Highlands in the shuffling pace with which the deputation returns home:

> They gaze at the closed doors like uncomprehending sheep, then slowly they turn and wind down the sweep of avenue, like mourners at a funeral, no longer like marching soldiers.[9]

Nor does the Kirk's collusion in the Clearances, or the aristocratic and middle-class perspectives it is seen to represent, escape censure. Mr Cameron, the Minister of Inchbuigh, is presented as the antithesis of his flock, separated from them by class, cultural background and even language. He has 'a clipped voice, different from the others in timbre and accent', and, in keeping with the conventional hierarchical order of literary language, he uses standard English with Biblical phraseology, whereas the Highlanders' lower social status is registered by their use of a demotic linguistic form. Nevertheless, in his exchange with the 'invisible' Callum, who is hidden inside the wooden settle, this generally-accepted convention, and, indeed, the Minister's own worth and that of the Church and social classes he represents, are all subverted by the juxtaposition of the clergyman's self-interested casuistry with the more rational, practical suggestions of the supposedly-ignorant cowherd. Thus, the reader is encouraged to look at the Clearances from an altered perspective, and in so doing, perhaps, to question the veracity of other historical narratives by which social and cultural elites explain and maintain their superior position.

When we think of Morrison's handling of the Clearances, it is important to recall that, when the novel was first published, there had already been calls for a new approach to Scottish history. In 1925, C. M. Grieve, the self-appointed architect of the movement now known as the Scottish Literary Renaissance, had issued just such a demand.[10] Until recently it has been commonly held, in reviews of Scottish literary history, that Neil M. Gunn's *Butcher's Broom*, published in 1934, was the first fictionalisation of the Highland Clearances to treat the subject from the perspective of the dispossessed Highlanders.[11] Indeed, Richard Price has argued that, prior to Gunn's novel, 'the centralist, elitist historiography of both the English and the Scots had rendered the whole episode a no-go area'.[12] As recently as 2006, in his introduction to the Polygon edition of *Butcher's Broom*, Kevin MacNeil makes the same claim, stating that it is 'worth remembering that at the time Gunn was writing this novel, there were no fictional antecedents'.[13] Yet *Breakers* predates *Butcher's Broom* by four years.

Similarly, credit for the castigation of the kirk's part in colluding in the Clearances has been attributed to the much later *And the Cock Crew* (1945) by Fionn MacColla and Iain Crichton Smith's *Consider The Lillies* (1968). While the episode of the evictions, although central to the plot, does not constitute the sole thematic focus of *Breakers,* I believe that its significance as the first fictional representation of this aspect of Scotland's past has been unjustly overlooked.

In its portrayal of Callum Lamont, Euphemia Gillespie's illegitimate son, *Breakers* also challenges earlier historical novels, such as Scott's *The Heart of Midlothian* (1830), which can be read as fictionalisations of Scotland's past, written in such a way that they made Scottish history appear to correspond to English – and Lowland Scottish – ideological imperatives. Morrison's novel appears to emphasise the fact that since our past informs our present, and since Highland and Lowland experiences have been vastly different, we cannot re-imagine and rewrite the history of one part of our nation to suit the ideological requirements of the rest. Nor can we simply omit events, movements or even ideas that run counter to the objectives of society's elites. Those unruly elements which cannot be contained within conventional historical narratives will, *Breakers* suggests, keep reappearing to trouble the 'comfortable' history employed by those in power to explain and justify their position. As in the prefatory definition of the word 'breakers', cause and effect cease to be viewed as part of a linear progression, and become a repetitive cycle of violent, destructive disruptions.

In her construction of Callum, Morrison attempts to forge a union between the Highlands and the Lowlands. From his Highland father, Duncan Gow, the farmer's son, Callum inherits an intuitive knowledge of the land. When he finds himself at Inchbuigh farm he realises that:

> ...the work came instinctively to him as though he had done it long ago and now all that he needed was to grow accustomed to it again. [And] [w]hen a whole litter of pigs died it was he who discovered that their beds had been made with bracken, but no one had ever told him bracken was poisonous to pigs.[14]

He is also superstitious, a characteristic commonly associated with the 'unenlightened' Highlander: 'He was not afraid of things but of the shadows that they threw; a curse would have haunted him more than any evil act he himself had perpetrated'.[15] And he is presented as taciturn, as befits those whose language had been denigrated: 'He took much longer than usual to learn to talk, but even after he mastered speech he was grudging with his words'.[16]

From his middle-class, Edinburgh-born mother he inherits an argumentative temperament and a rationality which does not match either his rural inheritance or his coastal upbringing. Like the rest of his mother's family he acts irresponsibly, particularly when he abandons Fiona Stewart, who believes he will marry her, and, also like them, he wants property, status and authority over others:

> Callum gazed down at where the bland farm-house was hidden behind a clump of trees, and his heart stirred within him. He had very patriarchal ideas. He would have liked a farm of his own with well-filled out-houses and flourishing crops and men to order about. [17]

But Callum is illegitimate; he is unwanted; he is a misfit. His development is hampered by the limitations imposed upon him by his circumstances and his environment, a point metaphorically conveyed in the physical effects of his cramped home at Stonemerns: 'He did not grow up slim and tall but broad-shouldered and thickset – as though the squat little cottage had not given him sufficient room for growth, and before he was in his teens he had the strength of a man'.[18] Even as a child, still unaware of his illegitimacy, he does not fit into the society in the coastal fishing village. He is introspective, and his psychological baggage makes him self-obsessed and suspicious:

> Even among these reticent, hard-working fisher-people he stood out as dark-browed and dour, 'ill to do wi'. He was suspicious and aggressive, with a head full of dimly-imagined wrongs. His thoughts all revolved around himself, heavy, cumbersome, complicated thoughts. He dwelt on them as a cow chews its cud.[19]

Typical of older representations of the Highlander, Callum is associated with vermin. This happens when Fiona catches a live rat as she tries to teach him to guddle for trout, and is suggested by the description of the barn where he has sex with Lillith: 'It was a dusty, ghostly place, with death-ticks beating in its rotten walls, ridden with mice and overrun with skuttling beetles'.[20] However, apart from fathering Lillith's sickly child, which eventually dies, he appears to play no lasting role in the Gillespies' future, since his death implies Lillith's eventual freedom to marry the lawyer, Napier Rand. Nor does his attempt to halt the Inchbuigh evictions help the Highlanders; the glen is cleared, and Joe, the most outspoken of the Stewarts, dies in the Lowlands, unable to cope with change. Initially, it would seem that, with his suicide, Morrison follows the convention of traditional historical fiction and writes the illegitimate Callum out of history. But this interpretation ignores both the manner of his death and the warnings of disruption and destruction that overlay the prefatory definition and are implicit throughout the novel's subtext.

Similarities between the two novels suggest that Scott's *The Heart of Midlothian* can be read as a palimpsest of *Breakers,* and this strategy takes us closer to what I argue Morrison was trying to do with the plot resolution.[21] Both Euphemias are unwed mothers, and daughters of men noted for their religious standing; although in Mr Gillespie's case it is a professional attribute rather than innate spirituality or doctrinal conviction. Callum, the illegitimate son, is in the same abandoned and eventually ostracised position as Scott's character, 'The Whistler'. Neither has been reared according to the social status of either of his parents, and, most significantly, neither is certain of having been baptised. This means that neither can lay claim to even the veneer of 'civilisation' which religious discourse, employed to underpin cultural imperialist interests, confers on the Christian community. Each grows up angry and alienated. In *The Heart of Midlothian* the Whistler's uncivilised behaviour leads to unconscious parricide, and because there is no place for someone like him in the new kind of Scottish society which Scott represents by the community at Rosneath, he is written out of the ending. He is removed from Scotland and sent to the colonies to live among the 'savages'. In *Breakers,* on the other hand, Callum's 'crimes' do not include murder, even though Lillith blames him for their baby's death. Apart from gratification of his sexual appetite, his only 'crimes' have been to try to force himself into a society that does not want him, and his attempt to change the course of history by preventing the evictions. Yet, within the logic of the plot, these would seem to be considered serious offences; Callum's futile attempt at the latter forces him back to Stonemerns to confront the fact of his illegitimacy: his success in the former is punished by his mental imbalance and eventual suicide. Not only does Callum question the Kirk's collusion in the extermination of the traditional Highland way of life, he dares to stand in the way of progress, and historical narrative convention demands that he is removed.

It initially seems that Morrison's handling of historical nonconformity is even more severe than Scott's, for not only does Callum die, but his progeny is weak and dies also. The threat implied by the verminous imagery appears eliminated. The possibility of an alternative construction of history would seem to be denied; middle-class values and conventional history appear to be reasserted. But such complicity with conventional ideology is subverted by the sympathetic portrayal of both Callum's situation and the symbolism implicit in the *manner* of his death. His drowning has been prefigured by repeated references to sea imagery throughout the text, for example, in the description of the cottage at Stonemerns: 'The rafters were made from the timbers of an old wreck, and before a storm at sea they creaked and groaned like a ship pulling at its anchor'.[22] The association is present also in his failed epiphanic experience:

> A tense, suppressed excitement mounted up in him, the opening in the sky gaped abnormally before his blinded eyes; he felt so powerfully colossal that the sea lay like a puddle at his feet.
>
> He waited, his breath indrawn, within an ace of omnipotent knowledge. The moment passed and he felt, creeping coldly between his toes, the ever-gnawing sea…[23]

Unlike Scott's plot resolution, which relies on the removal of extremes, Morrison keeps Callum's spirit closer to home by returning it to the sea. This strategy is particularly significant when we recall the Romantic associations of the ocean as 'the Almighty's form' and its use as a metaphor for power and freedom from social restraint.[24] Connotations of eternal movement and the restless energy of the sea, of which Callum's spirit is now a part, suggest not only the possibility of the continuity of this vital cultural force, but also the inevitability of repeated assaults by revenant, rebellious historical forces on the shores of supposedly 'civilised' Scotland.

Alongside this, we must also remember that Fiona Stewart, Callum's 'fiancée', remains as a live, physical force beyond the novel's ending. She is of pure Highland stock and is presented as a repository of its traditions. It is she who knows the true story of earlier unscrupulous, aristocratic land-grabbing at Gilhead. Had she inherited her rightful share of the farm, Callum, as her husband, would have been able to live the kind of life to which he was naturally suited. Their children would have followed them on the land, and the traditional Highland way of life would have been maintained. Fiona's unattractive appearance, ungainly manners and strange, almost incoherent speech do not prevent Callum from loving her, yet, she reminds the reader of Madge Wildfire, the aberrant female in *The Heart of Midlothian*, who was denied access to Rosneath's idealised Scottish community. In *Breakers*, not only does Fiona remain in Scotland, because she runs away and thereby avoids joining her family when they emigrate to Canada, but she also finds work as a housemaid in a middle-class household in the 'progressive' Lowlands, where her natural talents outshine those of her employers. Despite her earlier fears to the contrary, she discovers that 'it took a lot to kill Fiona Stewart'.[25] Significantly, too, with her 'stunted nose [that] was as red as a rowan' she is metaphorically linked with that tree's magical, protective properties,[26] an association that becomes especially relevant to her subversive role in the novel when we remember how Callum's father had told Euphemia that rowan berries could be preserved by burying them in a box until they were needed. It is Fiona, as the teller of traditional tales to Lowland children, who will preserve her own Highland culture, and pass on its traditions to others. And, when we recall how her final words are carried in the wind, and her sentence is left hanging unfinished in the air, at her departure from Callum, we realise that she has not been silenced, and that the full import of her prediction about the savage crushies may yet be felt.

Such sentiments would seem to have been given a new currency with recent shifts in Scotland's political scene. Devolution has encouraged a revisiting of our past, and a re-evaluation of our cultural inheritance. Until recently, many of our earlier literary endeavours had been allowed to lapse into obscurity, and works by Scottish women writers have suffered disproportionately in this respect. Apart from Canongate's reprint of *The Gowk Storm*, Morrison's work has been too long out of print. It has, therefore, fallen off the radar of many who teach and write about Scottish literature, as well as those who simply enjoy reading it. This new edition of *Breakers* is a major step forward in rectifying this situation.

Mary Seenan,
Skelmorlie
November 2008

Morrison, Nancy Brysson, *The Gowk Storm*. (1933 rpt., 1988) Edinburgh: Canongate.

2 McCulloch, Margery Palmer, 'Poetic Narrative in Nancy Brysson Morrison's *The Gowk Storm*' in Carol Anderson and Aileen Christianson, (eds.,) (2000) *Scottish Women's Fiction 1920s to 1960s: Journeys Into Being*. East Lothian: Tuckwell Press. pp. 109-119.

3 Hogg, James, (1824) *The Private Memoirs and Confessions of a Justified Sinner*, and R.L. Stevenson, (1886) *The Strange Case of Dr Jekyll and Mr Hyde*. See also Cairns Craig, (1996) 'The Body in the Kitbag' in *Out of History: Narrative Paradigms in Scottish and British Culture*. Edinburgh: Polygon. pp.31-63.

4 Swan, Annie S, (1890) *Sheila*. Edinburgh and London: Oliphant Anderson and Ferrier.

5 Morrison, Nancy Brysson, *Breakers*. (1930 rpt., 2008) Glasgow: Kennedy and Boyd. p.67.

6 MacKenzie, Alexander, (1883 rpt., 1994) *A History of the Highland Clearances*. Edinburgh; Mercat Press.

7 *Breakers*, (1930 rpt., 2008) p.53.

8 Ibid., p.62.

9 Ibid.

10   MacDiarmid, Hugh, (18.12.1925) 'The New Movement in Scottish Historiography: George Pratt Insh', *The Scottish Educational Journal*, collected in (1976) *Contemporary Scottish Studies/ Hugh MacDiarmid*, Edinburgh: 'Scottish Educational Journal'. pp. 68-70, cited in Price, Richard, (1991) *The Fabulous Matter of Fact: The Poetics of Neil M. Gunn*. Edinburgh: Edinburgh University Press. p.47.

11   Gunn, Neil M. (1934) *Butcher's Broom*. Edinburgh: Porpoise Press.

12   Price, Richard (1991) p.54.

13   *Intro to* Gunn, Neil M, (1934 rpt., 2006) *Butcher's Broom*. Edinburgh: Birlinn. p.x.

14   *Breakers*. (1930 rpt., 2008) p.42.

15   Ibid., p.41.

16   Ibid., p.35.

17   Ibid., p.52.

18   Ibid., p.35.

19   Ibid.

20   Ibid., p.117.

21   This approach owes much to the observation, originally made by Dr Carol Anderson, of the similarity between the situation of Euphemia Gillespie in *Breakers* and that of Effie Deans in *The Heart of Midlothian*.

22   *Breakers*. (1930 rpt., 2008) p.117.

23   Ibid., p.38.

24   Byron, 'Childe Harold's Pilgrimage', Canto Four, Verse CLXXXIII, in Robin Skelton, (ed.) (1964 rpt., 1989) *Selected Poems of Byron*. Oxford: Heinemann, p.57.

25   *Breakers* (1930 rpt., 2008) p.68.

26   Dating from the time of the Druids, the Rowan, or Mountain Ash, has been held to have magical properties; most notably, it was thought to provide protection against witches and other evil spirits. In Aberdeenshire, crosses made from rowan twigs were put over doors and windows to ward off evil spirits, and in Breadalbane a piece of rowan twig was tied to cows' tails to protect them from the 'evil eye'. In the context of its metaphorical use in *Breakers*, it is also significant that, according to folklore, an abundance of berries on the rowan foretells a bad harvest and/or a hard winter. See Gillies, William A. (1938 rpt., 2006) *In Famed Breadalbane*. Ellon: Famedram. p.352; McNeill, F. Marian. (1959 rpt., 1989) *The Silver Bough*. Edinburgh: Canongate. p.84; Henderson, L and Cowan Edward J, (2001) *Scottish Fairy Belief: A History*. East Linton: Tuckwell Press. p.104.

Book One

Chapter One

AT the beginning of March they left the house where all four children had been born. They left the apple tree in the garden, and the Whyte children next door, and the large, friendly congregation which papa had found so great a strain. It was such a pity, thought mamma, staring unseeingly out of the carriage window as the horses settled into a steady trot, that he differed so with all his assistants. But now, she comforted herself quickly, for she always made the best of things, that difficulty was over. With a congregation not an eighth the size of the one he was leaving, there would be no need of an assistant. Nevertheless, she sighed heavily and unconsciously, for each new house she went to was smaller than the one she had left.

None of her relations had anything in common with William Gillespie and they could not understand why she had married him. Indeed, when they came to think it over, Gillespie, who was always full of old saws, seemed to have nothing in common with anyone. Yearningly he looked back on yesterday, hopelessly he thought of to-morrow, while today wasted and died at his feet. And Ann of all people, who might have married anyone ...

To marry him she had left her childhood home, Number 13 Pardle Square. It was a fine old Edinburgh house built in the expensive, massive, elaborate style of its period. She could remember mamma in the vast, gloomy front bedroom, looking like a flower in a mausoleum, and papa coming up the steps in his coloured waistcoat. She also had a dim memory of a host of relations who had come to visit her parents. Large faces, framed in bonnets or bristling with beards and moustaches, had loomed with frightening suddenness at the children as they lay in their cots. Uncles had given them fourpenny bits and fond aunts had traced in Richard's diminutive features impossible likenesses to Grandpapa Quinn, who would have been so proud ...But they were all gone, those rustling, cooing relations, only the great empty house remained peopled by two middle-aged men, her brothers Richard and Tom.

Richard was the relation she always turned to when she wanted money, Tom when she wished advice. He, dear soul, would have given her money had he had it, but like her he was always in debt. Both brothers had been left the same income by their father, but while Richard had increased his portion, Tom had sadly depleted his. Richard's appearance suggested he prefaced everything, even business, with silent prayer. Tom looked as though he had lived every moment of his life and enjoyed it. Tom was a living monument to Richard of what not to become, and Richard was the formidable example to Tom of what he himself might have been had he taken all his elder brother's advice.

The manse in which Ann Gillespie had started married life at the beginning of the nineteenth century had been quite different from Number 13 Pardle Square, but she was a woman of resource and endless energy. Only big things interested her. Her large brain, so incapable of meting out the household money and grasping the grocer's monthly account, was deft at calculating how much it would cost to found an Orphans' Home. She worked on an ample canvas, counted in pounds and let the pennies go—a dangerous characteristic for an impecunious minister's wife. But through everything—disappointments, the increasing lack of money, her husband's illnesses—there beamed like four lanterns her four children. No longer did she sigh when she studied her face in the glass and realized that years were passing, for no longer did she study herself. She lived for her children and lived again in them.

What would it be like, she wondered, this new manse to which they were going, which took two days to reach and which was a mile from any other habitation and situated on the edge of a Highland Loch? It was so small, and William of course had to have a study where he could write his sermons, which left only one room to serve as parlour, drawing- and dining- room. The congregation, too, would be quite different from the one they had left. It seemed a farm was the only big house amongst a scattering of whitewashed thatched dwellings.

Her husband, seated opposite her, was referring to two books he held open in his hands.

"There seems to be some confusion about the date of the church," he was saying. "Wright says the middle of the eighteenth century, but you never can depend on Wright—he merely sweepingly asserts and never substantiates."

He shut one book with a bang and Euphemia, his youngest child, started. He plucked the spectacles from his nose. "That boy," he said, nodding over at his dozing son, "is sleeping with his mouth open again. When *will* he learn to breathe through his nose?"

They arrived at their destination the following day. They had to descend from the carriage on the high road and walk through a small wood down a winding, precipitous path to the edge of the Loch. The manse, surrounded by a wild, wet garden, stood a little apart from the church. Even when their furniture was in it and they had been living there for years it still looked empty from the outside. It was quite unlike any house Ann Gillespie had ever lived in before. Most of the ceilings were cam'ceiled, the doors squeaked when they opened and shut, and loose boards creaked on the stairs at the lightest footfall. Elizabeth wondered at first if the house were "taking to" them. It smelt of wet leaves and mould and sometimes, before or after heavy rain, the walls sweated. The sitting-room had the only chimney in the house that "drew," and Bella used to wind a scarf round Elizabeth's delicate throat to protect it from the damp.

It took the Gillespies some time to grow used to Bella. She had all the eccentricities of one who has lived too long by herself, for although she had been servant at the manse for years, deafness marooned her. She kept up a muttered conversation with herself and positively shouted when speaking to anyone. Her cap, attached to her head by one hairpin, sailed behind her in the wind, while her darting eyes gave the impression they were wildly trying to bring it back over her head.

Mrs. Gillespie did not know how she was going to manage. The only shops, a butcher's and a grocer's, were very small affairs at a distance of eight miles. But she did manage somehow. As the years passed she rarely left the manse, for it did not seem worth the trouble to put on her bonnet and cape only to go for a walk, and each time she climbed the path to the high road she found it steeper. So she remained inside, always occupied and sometimes preoccupied, while she pondered from where she could get sufficient money to send Alice on a long-dreamed-for visit to Edinburgh.

The only days that were not exactly like other days were Sabbaths and Wee Sabbaths. The Wee Sabbaths were Fast Days and on the ordinary Sabbaths there were long services to attend in the church which stood exactly halfway between Barnfingal and Auchendee. Each clachan had its separate graveyard, but they shared the same church. The Barnfingal portion of the congregation sat on one side and the Auchendee on the other. The minister's deep pew stood in an impartial position. Two elders were chosen from the Barnfingal side and two from the Auchendee, and the minister had to be careful at meetings to address each first in turn. There were no stained glass panes which one could look at with squeezed-up eyes and make go round and round in wheels of colour. The windows were certainly a queer, pointed shape, but they were so overgrown with ivy they were scarcely seen and were no good as windows. There was nothing to do to relieve the tedium of sitting for hours in the same stiff, pin-and-needle contracting position except to count whether the Barnfingal congregation beat the Auchendee one, or whether there were more men than women in the church. It did not take one more than a few moments to tot up the children, but they were misleading, for many of them were so small they were almost swallowed by the high pews.

So the years slipped past almost covertly, swift springs and hasty summers gave place to prolonged autumns and winters, until Euphemia was seventeen and Alice the magical age of twenty-one. Glen was nineteen and his father had begun to say that really something must be done with him, that when he had been nineteen he had been in the midst of hard study for his profession. But Glen was not the studious type, which perhaps was as well, for there was no spare money to send him to a university. Things dragged on a little longer until one day, when Mr. Gillespie's digestion troubled him more than usual, he said very emphatically a great many times that the sooner Glen was earning something to keep himself the better. Mrs. Gillespie, therefore, sat down at the writing-table and wrote to her brothers, asking them to help her to procure Glen some suitable post. She sighed as she wrote, for it seemed hard that she, born so generously to give, should always have to beg from others.

Chapter Two

THE firelight flickered on the figures grouped round the hearth, one minute hollowing and shadowing their young faces, the next throwing them into radiant relief. Their busy chattering had ceased and a stillness passed over them. Tomorrow the manse would seem so strange and unfamiliar when Glen was away; they could not imagine it without him. And Glen, gazing with unusual thought into the fire, reflected how strange and unfamiliar he would feel away from home. Everything in the house had suddenly become inexpressibly dear to him. Yet he had so often longed to go away, to know what lay beyond the Loch, what the silent, encircling mountains hid from him. But now on the eve of departure he felt tremulous, as a captive bird hesitates when its cage is opened.

It had been so difficult to believe that it was true; even when he had packed his bag it had just seemed like a delightful game of pretending something were going to happen. It was only that day at dinner, when Bella brought in a rhubarb tart made especially for him with a perfect rampart of pastry, that he realized he really was going. The realization gave him a hollow sensation and he felt that if anyone said a kind word to him he would burst into tears. He could not quite determine whether he were glad or sorry that after all it had not turned out to be only pretence.

"This time to-morrow," Euphemia said solemnly, "you won't be here."

She had made that remark at least twenty times at different periods during the day and only now did he find that her words annoyed him extremely. Euphemia always said the wrong thing at the wrong time.

"This time two years, I wonder what will have happened to us all," Alice said pensively.

"Nothing much, I should think," commented Elizabeth.

The door flew open and a minute later Bella appeared with their biscuits and hot milk. She banged the bumpy tray on to the table and disappeared as suddenly and as noisily as she had entered, drawing the door behind her with her foot.

Elizabeth hated milk but was made to take it by her father, who believed the more one disliked a thing the more good it did one. She was always eager to give her tumblerful in exchange for a parkin, but seldom found a willing bargainer. To-night, however, Glen drank it for her. He was in that quavering condition when he felt he would gladly have drunk quarts of milk if only it pleased someone.

Before going to bed he went to his father's room to bid him good night. Papa kept him so long reminding him of the various things he had forgotten to pack that it was eleven o'clock before he climbed the dark, creaking stairs to his room. He paused for a moment on the landing, overwhelmingly conscious of the house. They lived in it, they inhabited it, but it lived a life all its own. They could never influence it as it influenced them. Its heart-beats ticked in its walls, its windy breath could be felt in every room, it often sighed as though in pain. After all he was glad he was going, he told himself as he stood in the eerie dark.

When they had first come to the Barnfingal-Auchendee manse he had been small enough to thrust his head between the balustrades and not big enough to be able to pull it back by himself. It had been quite different from the house they had left behind them in Edinburgh. Glen's picture of his old home was very bright. All Glen's memories were bright, for he never allowed himself to penetrate into the dark corners of his mind where spooks and bogies lurked. It was so much pleasanter simply to pretend they were not there. The Edinburgh manse had in his memory a lustre and a richness it had lacked substantially in reality, but certainly it had been more comfortable and commodious than this one. Glen, who was very sociable, had such happy recollections of the numerous visitors who had come to see mamma. No one ever came to see them at Barnfingal.

He awoke too early next morning in a fever of excitement and snapped shut his bag which was crammed so full he could scarcely close it. The half-formed fear had taken possession of him that perhaps the house might not permit him to leave. He gulped down his breakfast as if afraid the carriage, which was ordered from Dormay, would come and go without him. At the last moment Bella reminded Mrs. Gillespie to give him his "lucky-cap" for protection. They all streamed up the path with him and packed him into the carriage as though he were an invalid, and kissed him good-bye over and over again, and told him to be sure to write....

His heart was wrung at parting from them, and he vowed to himself that he would make money, enough money for them all to do exactly what they liked with. It was not right his mother had to worry over bills and hide them from papa.... He leant dangerously far out of the window, and waved his hat until he no longer distinguished the individuals of the little group at the gate.

Chapter Three

"I LOATHE Sundays," moaned Elizabeth at the window, her head pressing on the pane.

"Come over to the fire and let's be cosy," Alice said briskly. "Put another piece of wood on, Euphie."

"It's two years ago exactly to-day since Glen went away," remarked Elizabeth after a pause, staring into the fire.

"The time's gone so quickly and yet so slowly," sighed Euphemia.

"It's the minutes that go slowly and the weeks that go quickly, I notice," said Elizabeth, "and Sundays always take twice as long as any other day to pass."

"Well, let's pretend what we would each choose if someone presented us with five guineas apiece to spend on a ball dress," suggested Alice.

"There wouldn't be much use of a ball dress," argued Euphemia, "when there isn't a ball to go to."

"I know," agreed Alice, "it would be provoking. We never go anywhere and we never see anyone except an occasional minister or a passing ploughman, and I think I almost prefer the ploughman—ministers are so dull."

"What about Mr. Bowden?" Euphemia took her up quickly.

Alice laughed. Mr. Bowden had once come to the manse when their father was indisposed and unable to take the services. He was a very young, pink man who, not without assistance, had become enamoured of Alice. On the night before his departure he had slipped a note under her door asking her to meet him on the moor the following morning. Alice, who never could keep anything to herself, had gleefully awakened her sisters to tell them about it. Elizabeth had been sleepy. Euphemia, scandalized, nearly rose to warn their mother, but on second thoughts decided not, knowing well that her sister would go if she wanted to, whatever their mother said. Mr. Bowden gave Alice a lock of his hair which she lost or—more likely —threw away before reaching home, and probably she had not thought anything further about him until Euphemia mentioned him now.

"Oh, he was dull and ordinary like all the others!" she exclaimed. "It was only hearing he was youthful and unmarried before I ever saw him that made him interesting."

"You found him interesting enough when you did see him," Euphemia said sharply, "and you have not behaved well towards him. You should not have met him on the moor if you were going to forget him as soon as he was gone."

"Nonsense!" her sister replied airily. "We have not heard of him since; he has forgotten me as I have forgotten him. Now, had it been you, Euphie, you would have taken him *au grand sérieux*— mooned about him by day and dreamed on his lock of hair by night. And when the months sped by and you heard no word from him, you would have gone into a decline and fashionably died. But no! no! I break my heart over no man—I let him do that for me!"

"Well," said Elizabeth, not troubling to disguise a yawn, "suppose we do what you were suggesting—about the ball dresses, I mean. You begin, Alice."

Euphemia would unburden her soul to anyone who cared to listen, and immediately Alice spoke one felt one had known her all one's life, but one never really knew Elizabeth, for she kept herself apart. She had the features of a Da Vinci Madonna, and in the clear eyes, which never coquetted or challenged like Alice's dancing ones, there dwelt something unfathomable, something akin to the inscrutability which baffles in the Mona Lisa. In the fragile body that one would have thought a breeze could sway lived a soul austere for her age which held unflinchingly to its laws of right and wrong.

"Well," said Alice, drawing her chair closer to the fire, "I would choose yellow, the golden yellow of daffodils. And the stuff would be flowered taffetas. For once in a way we would have them cut really low. I think—yes, I am sure—I would wear a fichu. I know they are quite out, but they are so becoming to one's shoulders. Now, Elizabeth, what would you have?"

"I," replied Elizabeth, "would choose pink."

"You would need to be careful," Alice said dubiously, "pinks are so dangerous."

"But my pink would be the most delicate shade imaginable," returned Elizabeth, "just white softly tinted. I wouldn't have it of taffetas, even though it's so fashionable, but of the finest sarcenet with dozens and dozens of flounces all edged with tiny rosebuds."

"Oh, I can see you!" cried Alice. Then her face grew wistful as she looked at her sister. "I wish you could have it," she said, "you would look so dear—you have such a tiny waist, Elizabeth," and she sighed. "What shape of neck would you have?" she asked, brightening. Alice dearly loved discussing detail in dress.

"Shoulder to shoulder," Elizabeth replied promptly, "with real lace."

"You forget," Euphemia put in chillingly, "that you have only five guineas to spend. You could not buy much real lace for that."

"Well," Elizabeth said calmly, "mamma would lend me hers, I'm sure. I mean the cobwebby stuff she had on her wedding-dress. It's much more beautiful than anything you could buy to-day."

"Mamma gives you everything," muttered Euphemia.

At that moment they were interrupted by their mother, who entered the room so full of breathlessness they all knew at once something had happened. Her face was puckered and troubled, and she sat down heavily on a chair as though unable to stand any longer.

"Why, mamma," asked Alice, startled, "whatever is it?"

"It's your father," began Mrs. Gillespie.

This information was received with impatience. It always was their father.

"Surely he can't say he's ill again," Alice said unfeelingly, "for he ate a quite excellent dinner."

"It's about Glen," went on Mrs. Gillespie.

"Glen!"

"Yes, your father has just heard. Mungo Malloch was coming from Dormay to-day and he brought the mail with him. And, you know, it's too unkind, your father says it's all my fault for being so weak with him. He always blames me for everything," she continued plaintively. "When you fell ill as children it was always my fault for not foreseeing and preventing it."

"Yes, yes, mamma, we know all that," put in Euphemia. "Go back to Mungo Malloch and the mail. Did he bring a letter from Glen?"

"Do let me tell it my own way, you always break my thread. I can't possibly say everything all at once. Yes, Mungo Malloch brought the mail and he's married."

"Who is? Mungo Malloch? But what on earth has that to do with us?"

"Don't be foolish, of course I didn't mean him. It was Glen we were talking about. He's married."

There was a pause of complete incredulity. Her daughters gazed at their mother unbelievingly. It was impossible, Glen could not be married. Why, he was only a little older than Euphemia and younger than Elizabeth. Their minds strove, and failed, to reconstruct mentally the irresponsible Glen into a married man. Alice was the first to recover from the shock.

"But, mamma, he can't be," she said protestingly. "In his last letter home he was asking papa to send him money for a new coat."

"I know, and unfortunately your father remembered that. He has such a horrid habit of remembering all the things you want him to forget."

"Who is she? Who is she?" Euphemia reiterated excitedly.

"He did write home about a Georgina Holmes," said Elizabeth. "I thought she sounded rather nice."

"He's written home about several," commented Alice, "and they all sounded rather nice. Glen married! It's fantastic. He hasn't grown up yet."

"Who is she? Who is she?" repeated Euphemia.

"We've never heard of her before," answered Mrs,Gillespie, "She is a Lucy Harley and she's English. That is really all he says about her." She looked a little hopelessly from one to the other of her daughters as though seeking desperately for a reassurance she knew she could not find.

"And what are they going to do?" inquired Elizabeth.

"That's what has upset your father so," returned her mother. "He's bringing her here."

"Here? To the manse?"

"Yes, he says he does so want us to meet her."

The pause that followed was broken by Alice, who said in lowered tones :

"In other words, he has nowhere else to take her."

Chapter Four

WILLIAM GILLESPIE was a minister but he was not a spiritual man; it is doubtful if he ever thought of God except as an elusive subject for his sermons. His two hamlet congregations did not keep him busy, and for hours at a time he read. His books grew too numerous for his shelves and lay banked against the walls, their second-hand bindings neatly mended, their loose leaves tidily gummed in, their yellowing pages pencilled with methodical notes and spidery interrogation marks. He read about the ice age, about folklore, old buried cities and ancient lake dwellings, about dead civilizations, and lost tribes.

As the years passed God became more and more unreal. His sermons were always hackneyed and dull, but when he was in the mood his conversation was interesting, for he could talk on any subject. Sometimes he would take his daughters and show them where, among the wild hills, there was what looked to him like the grown-over mounds of a one-time Roman encampment. Or he would point out how a small wooded knoll had been shaped with ice, or trace with his stick the fossil of a leaf in a rock. Sometimes he would even rouse himself out of his depressed preoccupation to joke with them. Gazing at the dazzling beauty of his eldest daughter, he would promise them they would all have a holiday or go abroad for a time "when Alice marries her duke." To which Alice would retort, "You introduce me to the duke, papa, and I'll do the rest."

When their absent son's name was mentioned, Mrs. Gillespie's eyes would grow misty and she would think of him as a little boy running into her room and telling her that he was feeling "so boundy" that morning. Or she would see him again as her darlingest baby with an adorable curl in the middle of his forehead. He used to sit so still while she brushed a lock of his hair over her first finger and then carefully withdrew the finger ...She never missed anyone so much as she missed Glen, and Bella would try to comfort her by saying, "He's bad wha's never missed."

But their only son had always been a thorn in his father's side. The boy lacked the verve of his sisters which Mr. Gillespie, who had very little spirit himself, secretly admired. He was irresponsible and incorrigible and, to his exacting parent, idle. Mr. Gillespie was forced to compare him most unfavourably to what he himself had been when young.

Despite his father's gloomy predictions, Glen seemed to progress quite well in London, for after six months he was removed to a higher department in the shipping office and received a slight rise of salary. His gay, unforced manners and youthful enthusiasm made him universally popular, and he never lacked companionship. His infrequent letters home contained more about small sociabilities than his work, as Mr. Gillespie pointed out to his wife. Otherwise his father had nothing to grumble at except his requests for small sums of money over and above the annual allowance, for Mr. Gillespie had quite forgotten to include such necessary items as clothes when he had calculated how much his son would cost him in London.

Then Glen, without even consulting his father, had abandoned his slow but sure post in the shipping office and taken up insecure journalism. His apologetic requests for money now became urgent demands. Mr. Gillespie had the morbid satisfaction of a spey wife living to see her unwelcome prophecies fulfilled.

Papers began to arrive at the manse containing articles and stories signed one Owen Cholmondely. Mrs. Gillespie read them with proud tears in her eyes and kept them in her untidy wardrobe.

Probably to impress his father, Glen unwisely wrote that he received two or three guineas for them. Mr.Gillespie, who immediately stopped his allowance, was baffled. He could not understand how any editor paid some pounds for what struck him as inconsequent, romantic nonsense. And only last week Chambers' Journal had returned to him "The Strata Formation of the Loch Tarrol District" which had taken him over a month to write and which was closely packed with weighty, noteworthy facts.

Then, just when the distant Glen had clothed himself in a remnant of respect, he married. Mr. Gillespie could not get over that. Not only was the young owl married but he was bringing his bride to the manse. His letter heralding their approach was so timed that when it was received in Barnfingal he and his wife had left London and were on their way to Scotland. That, Mr. Gillespie thought, mouthing in his irritation, was so like Glen.

Chapter Five

ELIZABETH hurriedly finished a cross-stitch toilet-set she had been making for her mother's Christmas present and put it in the spare-room. Alice contributed her one and only bottle of scent and Euphemia darned the bed-hangings so beautifully her darns had the appearance of a pattern.

"It still looks shabby," she sighed as the three of them stood in the doorway on the afternoon they expected their brother and his wife.

"It's more faded-looking than shabby," said Alice, "like someone who might once have been pretty."

"I wonder why mamma chose walnut when she could have had Jacobean with twists," commented Elizabeth.

"I like light furniture best," Euphemia said.

"I don't," replied her sister." Dark furniture reflects everything nice twice and makes even ugly things lovely."

Euphemia walked to the window.

"They should be here any moment now," she said restlessly.

They went downstairs into the living-room to wait beside their mother, whose presence filled every room she entered. As full of the zest for life at fifty as she had been at fifteen, she was a woman of dauntless courage, who always looked forward to some radIant day to dawn when all their ships would sail triumphantly home, heavy laden. In her handsome face there flickered the shade of each of her children, but none possessed the nobility of her fine features. "They had noses in our day," Bella had once said to her. It was from her side of the house, as she repeatedly remarked, that her family inherited its good looks.

She gazed from one to the other of her daughters that afternoon as though trying to see them as an outsider, such as Lucy Harley, would who saw them for the first time. All her children were tall, she thought proudly, and had small bones and long legs. Euphemia sat in a low chair gazing into the fire. She was the one who was most like her father. Her dark eyes were too large for her thin face and she looked older than Alice. Mrs. Gillespie always wished an artist could see Alice, although no portrait of her eldest daughter would have done justice in her eyes to that sparkling, vivid beauty. No brush, however swift, could catch the liveliness of expression, the grace and charm of her daughter's face. She glanced at Elizabeth leaning back in her chair and as quickly looked away.

Elizabeth was so unlike Alice they might never be taken for sisters, but Elizabeth was every bit as pretty in her own way—even prettier some might say, mused Mrs. Gillespie. She was lovelier as the figure in a portrait is lovelier than the living one who gazes on it, or as a reflection is lovelier than the reality.

The bewildering by-ways and sidewalks their mother took to reach a given point in conversation often made her young listeners impatient. Elizabeth had once remarked that she would not like to get lost in mamma's mind. Now her thoughts drifted from her daughters to her son and his unwelcome, unknown wife. She fretted for a moment or two about a hole in Euphemia's stocking which Euphemia said no one would notice unless they were told but which Mrs. Gillespie thought most conspicuous. She pondered on whether Mrs. Gow, the farmer's wife, had meant to be rude that morning or had been merely tactless. She groped for a space amongst long-ago childish memories for a quotation in a copybook about tact and kind hearts. Copy-books made her think of her old home in Edinburgh and of Richard and Fanny and dear Tom who was so like herself and liked the best of everything. Then, sighing a little, she thought of her husband and hoped he would not be too hard on Glen. The boy was so young and she was sure, in her prejudiced maternal way, that it had all been Lucy Harley's fault.

"Here they are," Alice said suddenly.

They entered in a whirl of talk and air. Glen was the same as ever, as gay, handsome and as charmingly egotistical as of old. One always felt that happenings to him were of so much more importance than happenings to oneself. He was perhaps a little nervous at the first—not because of the impression his relations would make on Lucy but because of the impression she would make on them.

The frightened eyes of the sister-in-law moved from one to the other, taking stock, while her pouting mouth made her look as though she were going to cry at any moment. She came to the conclusion that there was something unusual about each of them and allowed her gaze to rest on Glen as though to reassure herself. Alice was much the prettiest, she told herself, and she thought she liked her best. She felt she could quarrel quite easily with Euphemia. She was most interested in Elizabeth, who was Glen's favourite, but she did not quite know what to make of this girl with the slender hands and delicate, blue-veined skin. Even Alice looked too blooming beside her fragile sister.

The sister-in-law was small, with mouse-coloured hair and brown eyes—just exactly what a Lucy should look like, Alice thought. Why Glen had become attracted to her, she could not perceive, but then Glen was very susceptible and prone to extract excitement from every available source.

When he first came upon her, Lucy had been living on the bounty of a bachelor uncle and a maiden aunt who only believed in pleasure for the young in very limited doses. Having great difficulty in even catching sight of her, she had become to Glen as unprocurable and desirable as a fairy princess guarded by two tyrannical dragons. He was only able to arrange a few stolen meetings. Lucy's breath was completely taken away by this princely, ardent young man who had come so startlingly into a life she had never expected to be other than drab and uneventful. Their love flamed to fever-pitch, as a fire is flamed by opposing winds.

Lucy at last tearfully agreed to be secretly married, but at the back of her mind she never dreamed it would transpire. Secret marriages somehow did not seem to happen nowadays in this world of Uncle Benjamins and Aunt Mattys. But everything went perfectly smoothly, almost as though the fates themselves had taken the matter in hand and determined there would not be one hitch. Uncle Benjamin went to Wolverhampton on business and on the very day of the wedding Aunt Matty retired to a darkened bedroom with one of her sick headaches. When she came downstairs on the following evening she was confronted by a tall, fair young man whom her niece affirmed was her husband. Lucy was a little dazed, for she could not recover from her surprise that she felt exactly the same now she was married as she had felt single.

What followed made her feel more dazed. As they were assuring Aunt Matty that of course they would tell Uncle Benjamin she had nothing to do with it, the front door banged. It was Uncle Benjamin home earlier than expected from Wolverhampton, where his business had gone badly. The fates had now evidently lost their interest in Lucy's affairs.

Being greeted by his married niece and a new nephew did not improve Uncle Ben's irascible, uncertain temper. But the louder he talked, the more loudly Glen talked back at him and the smaller Lucy tried to make herself. Never had she admired her splendid Glen so much. The climax came when Uncle Ben accused Glen of marrying Lucy for his, Uncle Ben's, money. After that Lucy made up her mind that never, never could she forgive him—no, Aunt Matty, not if he lay dead before me.

Glen, biting furiously at his thin lips, shouted back that he loved Lucy and had married her for love alone, that he had never known her uncle had money, and if he had he would have known that he would damn well keep it for himself. And Uncle Ben, looking very ugly, had sneered over the table, "Let love support you then." Glen had retorted they would not stay a night in such a house, and when it was snortingly pointed out to him that they had never been invited, he had magnificently forbidden Lucy to take away anything but what she stood in. Indignantly he took her to the house of one of his friends, and it was from there that eventually he wrote to his father.

Aunt Matty remarked after they were gone that other people's children were not like your own, and Uncle Benjamin took out his will, which was very much altered and initialed owing to the delinquencies of the various legatees. He struck Lucy out of it altogether. Aunt Matty watched him glintingly over the top of her spectacles and her knitting-needles clicked with a renewed rapidity and precision.

Chapter Six

IT was rather difficult when one was only twenty-one, and not a very sophisticated twenty-one at that, to remember one was a married man. In his own home amongst his own people, who had become individuals once more now he was with them, laughing again over the old familiar stories, Glen was apt to forget there was such a person as Lucy. Then her silence would be borne in upon him, and he would suddenly kiss her a great many times on her soft cheek and call her endearing names. As the days passed Lucy was seized with an unreasonable jealousy. She did so hope Mr. Gillespie would come to some decision about what was to be done with them, and she did so hope he would come to it soon. She wanted to go away, to get Glen away before he became a part of this house and a part of his family again. There was an attraction about even the shabby manse with its atmosphere of what she could only describe to herself as its "fallingdownness." At least it made one feel that one's favourite pink and white was after all rather an ordinary scheme for a bedroom. She wanted a little home of her own, cosiness and Glen all to herself. She did not belong here, but he did. She might even lose him here—one could lose a person even although one went on living with them in the same house. Already she thought she noticed a change in his attitude towards her; he was not so careful of her, so gently commiserating as he used to be.

His father did talk the matter over with Glen. Mr. Gillespie quite enjoyed talking matters over even although he went round and round in a circle and was at the end of the same opinion as he had been at the beginning. Lucy was sometimes at these conferences, but she was disturbing to her father-in-law's train of thought. When he gave little incidents of Glen's infancy to portray how even then he could not be depended upon, she would clap her hands and cry delightedly, "The little darling! The little darling! Oh, do tell me that again, Mr. Gillespie."

At last, after ten days of prolonged discussion, the minister impatiently asked his son if he had anything constructive to suggest. To Lucy's horror she heard her husband propose they should stay at the manse for a time while he wrote his stories and carried on with his journalism. Lucy, who was highly strung, nearly screamed at such an idea. She interrupted wildly to say that would never do at all. Did dear Glen (who was now thoroughly irritable) not see that he could not write topical articles in the heart of the Highlands and he was paid so little for Nature notes. Oh, it always took so much out of one to make Glen realize things, but she clenched her hands until her knuckles whitened and told herself she must not permit such a thing. It was not only her jealousy of his family which made her so definite. She knew her darling Glen just well enough to realize that he would be quite content to drift on at the manse for years.

Mr. Gillespie then said, what he had said so often before, that he could not be expected to keep up two households on a stipend not sufficient for one. The only thing he could suggest was for Glen to go to Edinburgh to see his mother's relations and ask them to procure him some post. In his spare time he could work at his articles until he had an income which allowed him to set up house with his wife. Meanwhile Lucy could, if she wished, remain at the manse.

Glen did not like this prospect at all. He told himself it was because he would be separated from Lucy, but in reality he dreaded meeting his uncles when he had so casually thrown up the previous post they had found him. To his astonishment, however, Lucy sided with his father. Blinking back her tears, she said she supposed that was the only thing they could do. When he announced very emphatically that he could not live without her, she promised she would write to him every day and that she would begin to sew for their little house. "So that," she pursued, standing on tiptoe and gazing almost searchingly into his face, "when you make a home for us, I shall have everything ready to put into it. I'm sure," she added in her practical way, "Euphemia will do all the hem-stitching for me."

There was no reprieve for Glen. He could not wriggle out of the meeting with his disapproving Uncle Richard and the debonair Uncle Tom whose negligent attitude always seemed to imply, "Go and drown yourself but don't come boring me about it."

He left one morning for Edinburgh and returned to the manse some days later. His uncles, he informed his family, could do nothing for him in Edinburgh, but if he went to London they could procure him a post with fairly good prospects. Really, he said to himself, it served Lucy right. Now she would not have him for even an occasional week.

So one wild morning Glen left Barnfingal in a raging wind and a blatter of rain which quickly blotted him from view, and Lucy was left in the queer house she distrusted so much, where anything might happen.

She had been born and bred in London. This place with its dead-looking green hills rising one behind the other filled her with an unutterable melancholy. Everything about it, the mountains, the hills, the Loch, was so eternal that one felt if one's little life suddenly stopped it would not matter at all. They would still be there.

Tall, unpruned trees grew so near the house that some of their branches even touched the windows. In summer, when the sun filtered between the leaves, a glimmering reflection was thrown into the uncurtained rooms which gave them the impression of lying under water. But now there were no leaves on the trees. Black-limbed they stood. At night, when there was a moon, they threw shadows on the darkened window-panes.

Elizabeth loved these shadows. She did not sleep well and would lie watching their ever-restless tracery. There was a twig on a certain bough, and as it moved across the window it looked to her like the form of a little praying priest. Alice was the only person she let into this precious secret.

But Lucy hated the shadows. If she gazed at them for long she saw faces form, evil faces with snouts. Sometimes the shadows would become frenzied, when the gaunt trees seemed as though possessed of devils, and the priest would swoop across the pane. Lucy had never heard anything like the wind. She did not know whether she disliked it more when it stormed or was hollowly monotonous. She could not bear to listen to it and would muffle her head with the sheets. Even then she heard it and would weep until she slept out of sheer exhaustion. Sometimes the storms lasted for days at a time. Pieces of leaves stuck, as though gummed, to the wet window-panes; the threadbare rugs flapped like live things with the draught blowing from underneath the doors. When one put out a trembling hand in the dark to light a friendly candle, the tiny light would be maliciously blown out. And one would remain very still, one's heart beating with terrifying irregularity.

She prayed that if she ever had a child it would not be born in this house. If it were she felt it would belong to it, not to her, would be doomed from its birth for misfortune.

Altogether life was not very bright at the manse just then. Their sister-in-law moped all day. Euphemia kept bursting into tears for no apparent cause. Mr. Gillespie feared he was ill and retired to bed. Mrs. Gillespie said she would have to write to the Presbytery once again to ask them to send a minister to take the services on Sunday.

Chapter Seven

The temporary minister was standing in the rain paying the man who had driven him from Dormay. All the other temporary ministers had been young and had walked the eight miles' distance, carrying their scanty luggage. But this man was not young and his pieces of luggage were so numerous that the carriage was a necessity. He stood, tall and distinguished, in his well-cut clothes. When he turned to enter the manse his face was plainly visible to the young Gillespies who were watching his arrival from an upstairs window.

"That," Alice said composedly, "is the man I'm going to marry."

"But," reminded Euphemia, who had been unable to procure a good view, "I thought you always said you would never marry a minister because it is such a disadvantage having a man in the house all day."

"I've changed my mind," Alice said airily," but I shall make it quite clear, of course, that I'm not interested in Sunday schools or missions."

"He's quite elderly," commented Lucy in her unimaginative way, "and probably has a wife and a large family."

"That is never a married man," Alice declared.

Tea-time that afternoon proved quite delightful. Mrs. Gillespie and the temporary minister, Francis MacMillan, made up little conversational bouquets and threw them to each other over the tea-cups. He stood with his back to the fire, his benign brow bent, and his rather preoccupied eyes looking from one to the other of the faces below him. He told Mrs. Gillespie they were the prettiest bunch of flowers he had ever seen gathered in the one room, 'pon his word they were. He was not married, Alice skilfully discovered. Lucy secretly thought that if Mr. MacMillan had attained middle-age without being married, he would not be likely to change now, but it was not very long before he had separated the eldest Miss Gillespie from her sisters and from the round and dimpled sister-in-law.

Mr. Gillespie still remained indisposed in bed and the temporary minister stayed at the manse much longer than had at first been expected. Every morning, rain or sun, he went for what he called his "constitutional." When it was dry the girls accompanied him, and it was always Alice who walked buoyantly at his side. The country was looking its saddest. The gallant iris leaves were bent and tipped with brown, the winding path from the manse to the road was sodden with wet leaves which muffled their footsteps. The sky was monotonously grey and the wind piercing and raw, but to Alice the walks were never long enough.

They were all charmed by Mr. MacMillan, even Lucy agreed he made a most pleasant companion. He was a handsome man with a powerful physique, but his striking face had no subtleties of expression. His quite ordinary sentences were delivered in so impressive a manner they became weighty and were heard with respect. Alice learnt to become a most attentive listener. Only to Elizabeth, with her rather painful penetration, did she seem like one so taken up with tap-tap-tapping at a door that she did not yet realize no one was behind it.

One afternoon Elizabeth was sitting alone in the living-room wondering where on earth Euphemia could be. Lately she had gone away by herself for long periods at a time. This was unlike Euphemia, who hated to be alone and always liked a companion even if only to contradict. Also for some time past she had been very pent up, but everyone thought that was because she was anxious about their father's health. Elizabeth was wondering if this really could be the reason when her sister hurriedly entered the room.

"I was thinking about you, Euphie," she said through the dark. "Light the lamp, will you?"

"No," Euphemia replied, "let's just stay as we are," and she came and sat down at the fire.

"Elizabeth," she said suddenly, "I have something terrible to tell you."

The other did not reply, but she noticed her sister's hands were clasped convulsively in her lap.

"Do you remember," she pursued with difficulty, as though each word were being dragged unwillingly from her, "Mrs. Gow said— said something to mamma long ago, before Lucy came, about— about my having once been seen with her son."

"Well," Elizabeth replied calmly, "you couldn't help that, could you? It was on the king's high road."

"The Gows didn't like it," Euphemia continued desperately, "they were trying to warn me through mamma. But it was too late. Oh, Elizabeth, do understand."

The silence became oppressive. A chair neither was sitting on creaked. The ticking of the clock grew strident.

"You are quite sure?" Elizabeth asked at last.

"It's the only thing I am sure of," said Euphemia, and she covered her eyes with her hands as though trying to blot from them the memory of a ruined mill which stood beside the brawling burn.

"Mamma must be told," Elizabeth said slowly.

"Yes, yes, but not papa—I would die if papa knew. Elizabeth, you tell her."

"I'll tell her if you want me to. But afterwards papa will need to know."

"How? He won't. Oh, swear on your oath you won't tell him or Lucy or Glen."

"No, no, of course I won't. But when it's born, you'll—"

Euphemia shuddered spasmodically.

"I hope it's dead," she whispered huskily. "I hope it never comes. I——"

"But supposing," went on that unhurried voice, "it should come—what then?"

"It can be boarded out somewhere." There was a pause before Elizabeth answered and her voice when it did speak sounded very far away.

"Ah, that makes it easier then, doesn't it?" The door was suddenly burst open and light streamed into the darkened room. Alice stood in the doorway with Lucy behind her. To Euphemia, hysterical and superstitious, it seemed symbolical that she sat in the dark while her sisters stood in the light. She was as apart from them as a changeling is separated from its more fortunate foster brethren. Her heart was heavy with bitterness as she looked at them. There was the radiant Alice who walked as though she were not earth-bound. She would probably marry Francis MacMillan, who would give her a home, position, security. There was Lucy, who was happily married to Glen, and Elizabeth....She almost envied Elizabeth most of all, who was in this world but so oddly not of it.

Her sisters tried to make no difference but, Euphemia thought resentfully, there was a difference. She felt it, and so did they. The only one who was exactly the same was her mother. Mrs. Gillespie's mind was a piece of exceptional machinery which rejected everything that was not fit for easy consumption, retaining only what was palatable. When Elizabeth told her, there flashed before her the memory of Mrs. Gow's flushed, worried face when she had jerkily spoken to her that summer morning some months ago. But she bore up under the shock much better than anyone had expected. She had never failed any of her children and she did not fail Euphemia now. The only question she asked was whether or not her daughter wished to marry Duncan Gow, but the very mention of his name now made Euphemia shiver. She agreed, therefore, that papa should not be told. Euphemia, she said after a night's troubled thought, must go to Betsy Lamont, an old servant of Mrs. Gillespie's childhood days, who lived at a place called Stonemerns.

Papa was told that Euphemia must go away for a change as it was feared she was falling into a decline. Papa's suspicious nature did not allow him to accept this information without questioning. He spoke to Dr. Wegg about it the next time he came to visit him, but Dr. Wegg was old now and even in his youth had been absent-minded. Elizabeth was the one who had come most frequently under his care, and when Mr. Gillespie spoke of his daughter, Dr. Wegg not unnaturally thought he referred to her. Yes, yes, he agreed with Mrs. Gillespie, a change would be very beneficial for the child. Oh, well, decline was perhaps too harsh a word to use, but there was no denying that the manse was damp, and damp for little missy spelt disaster.

The day before Euphemia was to leave papa discovered that Stonemerns was at the sea. What, he demanded irately of his wife, was the use of sending the girl to the coast to escape damp? He was startled by his wife asking almost fiercely where Euphemia could go, then, where it cost them next to nothing? Mr. Gillespie, whose criticism was never constructive, was silenced.

The following day Euphemia left the manse. Alice did not deny to herself that she was glad to see her go. She had been in secret suspense in case Francis MacMillan guessed the real reason for her sister's sudden departure. Unconsciously she knew that the discovery would prejudice such a man as he against the whole family.

But MacMillan had no suspicion of anything being wrong and proposed to her, as she had expected, before he left Barnfingal some weeks after Euphemia. It was arranged the wedding would take place within a year. He left more preoccupied than ever and returned to town. Before the May term, to all their neighbours' startled surprise, the Gows gave up the farm where they had lived for years. They went much farther north to a place no one in the district had ever heard of before. The Marquis of Moreneck's grieve did not fill the farm with another tenant, for the Marquis of Moreneck wanted his lands now for deer and sheep. Those clachans that were not being swept away at one time were being slowly weeded out until there were more deserted, ruined cottages amongst the hills than whitewashed, thatched dwellings.

Chapter Eight

STONEMERNS was a small collection of cottages standing bleakly on wild moors. The fishing quarter of the village comprised huddled, thatched dwellings, dirty and weather-beaten. The few remaining houses were squat stone cottages. With their deeply-set windows and ugly lines they had been made solely to keep out the elements and not in any way for beauty or comfort.

It was an unprepossessing village and no traveller would have cared to remain there longer than was necessary. But very few travellers passed through Stonemerns, for it was situated far from the high road and led nowhere. It had not even the thrill of being on the very edge of the coast. To reach the sea one had to walk nearly a mile over wearisome ploughed fields. There was no sandy shore and the fishermen had to spread their nets to dry on the shingle beside the crude harbour.

The wind was fierce and biting; it tore over the moors as though wishing to uproot them and penetrated into the coach where Euphemia sat, the solitary passenger. Every few minutes she peered through the pane into the swiftly gathering gloom. Snow had fallen and lay in the furrows of the prune-coloured ploughed fields, giving them a speckled appearance. Snow! Yes, and the week after next would be Christmas. The horror of how she was to spend it swept over her in waves of misery. Last year's Christmas stood out suddenly radiant and wondrously gay—all the rooms brightly lit and the table so beautifully decorated by Alice. They had not been able to procure any holly, but in the autumn they had preserved rowans by putting them into a box which they buried in the ground and did not dig up until Christmas. It was Duncan Gow who had told her to do that. God, if only she could bury in the earth all that had happened since and never need to dig it up again!

When she descended from the coach she was met by Annie Lamont, the daughter of Betsy Gaughan, who had been a servant to Mrs. Gillespie's mother. Annie's face was so shadowed by her bonnet that Euphemia could not see it. A faint light shone here and there between the chinks of shuttered windows as they walked down the gusty street. When they turned the corner the wind caught Euphemia's full skirts and swirled them round her legs. Her guide stopped at the last cottage and remarked in her flat voice that here they were. Euphemia had to bend her head as she entered.

Annie said she was sure Miss Gillespie would be tired and would like to go to bed at once. There was a nice fire in her room. She knew Miss Gillespie would excuse her mother not coming to greet her, but she was old now and rarely stirred from her chair. If she would like to see her, however, and did not mind coming into the kitchen, her mother would be so pleased.

Euphemia was shown an old, spectacled woman in a very white mutch and wrapped in a great many shawls. She smiled up at her guest and surprised the girl by talking quite intelligently to her. Somehow Euphemia had imagined that when one was old enough to have a daughter as elderly as Annie Lamont one would be nodding and senile.

Annie, tall and gaunt, led the way to the bedroom by the light of a candle. It lit up her face and revealed her to have high cheekbones, a bright colour and a big and bony nose— like the preposterous projection which sometimes forms on a candle. Startled, one looked at her a second time to refute or confirm one's first impression.

When she was left alone Euphemia gazed slowly round the room. It was scrupulously clean but very ugly. Everything was so scrubbed and of the coarsest, from the thick crochet curtains and antimacassars to the blankets on the box-bed. The room was icily cold, for the fire was poor and the floor was stone. But Euphemia dared not be critical. She leant her head against the mantelpiece and thought how terrible it must be to be like Annie, with her red hands, to whom a fire in a bedroom was evidently the height of luxury....

The sheets were rough and dragged on her knees and elbows; all the good had been washed out of the blankets long ago. They were heavy weights, devoid of warmth, pressing her down. She lay in bed trying to accustom herself to the unfamiliar sounds. Annie's feet made a nerve-wracking "clatter" on the stone flags. At last she heard her turn the ponderous key in the outer door and wind up the clock in the narrow passage.

After that the house was quiet—as quiet as a house ever can be to the only person who lies awake in it. Every hour, however, the silence was rudely shattered by the "lobby "clock, which had a startlingly loud china voice. Euphemia wished fretfully that Annie had forgotten to wind it. Outside the quietness was only disturbed by the footsteps of some late fisherman echoing down the cobbled street; they passed so near Euphemia's window that sometimes it seemed as though they were coming in. There was another sound, but it was so ceaseless it had become part of the silence. It was the monotonous murmur of the not far distant sea, which sounded hollow and muffled as the phantom sea in a shell when pressed to one's ear. It harassed Euphemia, for she wondered if she really did hear it or if she were only imagining she did. She wished the house had been either a little nearer, when it would have been more audible, or a little farther away out of earshot altogether.

It seemed to her that no sooner had she with difficulty fallen asleep than she was awakened. She frowned and restlessly turned on her other side. There they were again—clatter, clatter, clatter. What on earth was Annie doing up at this time in the morning? It was still dark as midnight—it must be long before six. Now she was scrubbing—really it was ridiculous—and now came the slap, slap of a wet cloth on the floor.

During the following days Euphemia never rose from bed, it was the warmest place in this cold house. She lay listening to the wind storming at the loose windows. With melancholy eyes she watched a long thread, dangling from a needle stuck in a pincushion, waving weakly, like a pennant, in the draught. Or she would gaze at the mottled reflection the water in the ewer threw upon the low roof.

She told herself she would never forget the goodness of Annie and her mother; they were the people who really mattered, those quiet, kind, sterling people. It was not so much what Annie did for her as the way in which she did it. Her attitude healed something in Euphemia that was wounded and hurt, and soothed her jaded nerves. Humbly Annie thought that what would have been very wrong and quite unpardonable for her to do was somehow not so wrong for Miss Gillespie. She wondered a little who the father was, a laird perhaps, or some titled gentleman....

Euphemia became very weak and Annie did her hair for her morning and night. It was such beautiful hair and there was so much of it, it took a long time to brush and comb. It was very fine and clung to the roughened fingers which so gently combed out what Euphemia called knots and Annie knew as "tugs".

The child was born late one night. No maternal emotion stirred in Euphemia when she saw it for the first time, no protective yearning welled up in her when she heard its helpless cry. It was much bigger than she had imagined a newly-born baby would be. And it looked so strong. She wished it were not so strong.

The doctor would not permit her to travel for some weeks. She bit her lip and nearly wept with vexation. She wanted to leave it all behind her as quickly as possible. From her bed she would watch Annie wagging her head at the baby, shaking her unbelievably long finger at it ...

At last she was well enough to leave. The remaining few days of waiting seemed the longest of all. She had a morbid terror something would happen which would prevent her departure; she was seized by a desperate, suffocating feeling that she was going to be tied here for life. But nothing did happen and the day on which she was to leave dawned uneventfully.

She went into the kitchen and said good-bye to Mrs. Lamont. For a moment or two she stood looking down at her baby as it lay in the creel beside the old woman. She put out her gloved hand and awkwardly touched its creased wrist. She felt something was expected of her but did not quite know what.

Annie went with her to the coach to carry her luggage. Euphemia found she had nothing to say to her. The coach took an eternity to come, so long she wondered frenziedly as the protracted moments passed if anything had happened to it. But it was only a few minutes late and drew up beside them with its snorting, impatient horses. Annie handed up the various pieces of light luggage to the guard and Euphemia entered the vehicle, which was fairly full.

She was returning to civilization, leaving Stonemerns and all that it contained behind her for ever. The coach jolted forward. She remembered to wave to Annie who stood, in her ridiculous bonnet, at the side of the road. Already Annie seemed dull and commonplace; Mrs. Lamont shrank back again into the obscurity of a kindly old servant of her mother's. The little stone house had become something sordid, for it was the cupboard which held her skeleton—a live skeleton with flesh on its bones, a large head and round, sloe eyes which stared blackly past her.

Book Two

Chapter One

HE was not the type of child one could caress, one was never seized by the desire to snatch him to one and hold him close. Sometimes when Annie looked down at him her heart misgave her, perhaps because of this. She could do so very little for him. Ridiculous though it was, she became almost timid of this tiny stranger who had been born under their roof.

He was very silent. He never gurgled or chuckled over hidden thoughts of his own, or blew bubbles or tried to catch his toes. He lay for the most part very still in his creel.

He took much longer than is usual to learn to talk, but even after he mastered speech he was grudging with his words. As he grew older Annie would come upon him standing motionless with his legs wide apart, his brow bent in preoccupation, as though he were evolving some intricate thesis in his large, unchildish head.

At other times he would gaze with such unblinking intensity into the fire that she would uneasily remove the piece of wood he was staring at and hastily mutter a prayer to break the spell of any evil spirits.

As he grew from a baby into a child, and from a child to a young boy, he betrayed no evidence of having a laird or a titled gentleman for a father, or even, for that matter, of his mother being a lady. One would never have picked him out as different from the other uncouth children who ran barelegged to school. He did not grow up tall and slim but broad-shouldered and thickset—as though the squat little cottage had not given him sufficient room for growth, and before he was in his teens he had the strength of a man.

Even amongst these reticent, hard-working fisher-people he stood out as dark-browed and dour, "ill to do wi'." He was suspicious and aggressive, with a head full of dimly-imagined wrongs. His thoughts all revolved round himself, heavy, cumbersome, complicated thoughts. He dwelt on them as a cow chews its cud.

He hated the sea, for he hated everything he felt he could not conquer. Its grey wildness filled him with dreariness and its ceaseless perpetuity weighed him with a sense of hopelessness. He had made up his mind very definitely that when he was older he would "get awa'," but he would get awa' across the moors and not across the sea.

He rose in the morning, pulled on his clothes and had a breakfast of hot porridge in the stone-flagged kitchen. Sometimes he would have to wait for his meal, when he would employ the time by squinting at the chalked floor, bringing it up to the level of his knees, then slowly letting it sink back again ... At school he was always allowed leadership amongst the other children because he was so rough and took by force what was not given him. In the afternoon he walked home alone, turning often on his way to view the dark, flat, moors behind him with their miles of straggling heather roots and stunted grasses.

At night he would stay in the kitchen until it was time to go to bed, while outside the darkness deepened and pressed against the window-pane. When the water in the kettle, swung on a swee, came to the boil, the lid opened and shut like a silently gasping mouth. In the wide chimney there were rumblings and miniature storms even in summer, as though the four winds of heaven were caught there and waged war against one another. The rafters were made from the timber of an old wreck, and before a storm at sea they creaked and groaned like a ship pulling at its anchor. When he heard that sound he always fidgeted in his seat in the chimney-corner until Betsy Gaughan would raise her head and tell him to "Be at peace there."

Be at peace ...how could one be at peace when one's thoughts wheeled and span in one's brain like birds with unwieldy wings, when they collected and accumulated like a scull of gulls, when their mustering from unknown quarters bewildered and frightened one? He wondered what it would feel like to be at peace, and once, as though to get the knowledge second-hand, he had gone into the overcrowded graveyard. Half the mounds had no stones marking them and in one corner stood a small haystack, for even grass was scarce at Stonemerns. The wind whistled over the low dyke and he left the place hurriedly, for he could not believe one was at peace when one's coffin mouldered under the cold earth and worms wriggled through ...

When he was twelve years old, he returned one day from school and informed Annie Lamont he was "no for going back." Annie received this thunderbolt in silence. She did not ask for his reason because she knew it was he now considered himself too old for lessons. Her heart beat uncomfortably at her side and her long thin fingers trembled as they placed articles on the wooden table for tea. She had realized that he could not be expected to attend school all his life, but she had put off considering what was to happen to him in the vague hope that things would "sort themsel's out". Now she was faced with fate in the shape of Callum sitting, frowning, with hunched shoulders at the fire.

What was she to do with him? Her unerring loyalty to the Gillespies forbade her to write and put the position before them; instinctively she knew Miss Euphemia would be of little help. Her remedy would be some pounds over and above the annual allowance, and Annie did not want any pounds. They were difficult to dispose of at Stonemerns and made little difference to the Lamonts who, if they had received a fortune, would have continued to shop with pennies. Annie knew that Miss Euphemia would resent being written to and that she would probably instruct her rather coldly to find him suitable work. But suitable work was scarce at Stonemerns. The fishermen did not want help, they had too many sons and grandsons of their own; and the farms, few and far between, were unproductive in that sterile country. Also Annie had a curious, almost guilty shrinking from seeing Callum coming home each night tired out after a hard day's manual labour. No, the only thing to do was to send him away.

Her mother dictated a letter to her which was sent to a distant cousin who lived inland some forty miles away. Hamish Gaughan was asked if he could find work on some farm for a strong young boy who was twelve years of age but who looked older. A month passed before they received any answer, but when Hamish did write it was to say he had procured work for the young boy as herd at Inchbuigh, a large farm in Gilhead.

Annie read out the letter to Callum and asked him almost wheedlingly if he would go. He was having a meal at the time and replied by an affirmative nod of his head, but he could hardly contain himself. In his excitement he nearly bit a piece out of his mug.

He went outside immediately after he had scraped back his chair from the table. He thrust his hands into his pockets to keep them warm and began to walk, for he felt he could not stay still. He walked with his eyes gazing on the ground and did not care whither his footsteps led him.

He was leaving it, this place he knew so well, with its humble dwellings and stench of curing fish. He was leaving the sea with its limitless wastes. The blood rose to his head and his pulses quickened. He felt he had been able to cheat the sea. He would not need to listen at night to the wind piping shrilly round the corner or hear it, hollow with space, as it blew across the water. He might even forget these sounds when he was somewhere else. Hamish Gaughan said it was a big farm and Callum loved big things. He felt as if one chain of many had been struck from him.

He found himself standing on a rock looking out to sea. The last time he had stood there was to watch them bringing Rob Tulloch's body to shore. They had rowed the boat from side to side so that no evil spirits could follow to steal his soul. He wondered what would have happened if they had not known to zigzag the boat ...

There were white holes and markings in the rocks like tiny skulls. Pieces of shell were stuck perpendicularly in the shingle like hundreds of little tombstones, and behind each the sifted sand was streaked like a long shadow. The pools were green and blue and dark purple and at the bottom sand moved perpetually and fronds of seaweed waved. The sky was oyster-coloured and there was an opening in the east like the mouth of a cave.

All around him was the emptiness of space, the wind swept the black hair from his brow. A tense, suppressed excitement mounted up in him, the opening in the sky gaped abnormally before his blinded eyes; he felt so powerfully colossal that the sea lay like a puddle at his feet.

He waited, his breath indrawn, within an ace of omnipotent knowledge. The moment passed and he felt, creeping coldly between his toes, the ever-gnawing sea ...

A few days later he left Stonemerns. Annie went with him to where the coaches stopped for passengers and where she had seen his mother ride away never to return. Now she and Callum did not wait for any approaching coach, for he was to walk to Gilhead. Neatly she turned back the cuff of his jersey which had fallen over his chapped hand and asked him if he had remembered everything.

"Good-bye, Callum, good-bye,"she said. "I'll miss ye sore, Callum—that I will."

She watched him walk along the winding moor road. He did not turn to wave to her, but she did not expect him to. She watched his retreating figure gradually and doggedly diminish until she lost it in the engulfing distances.

Chapter Two

THE country Callum walked into was much more to his liking than the stormy, barren country he had left. Both were wild, Stonemerns with the wildness of the sea and miles of flat, uncultivated moorlands, this country with bare mountains and burns brawling down their rugged sides. But the mountains did not fill him with the aching, unsatiated loneliness which the sea had done. No one could master it, lash it to their will. But he could imagine a king of the mountains, someone rather like them, brooding, black-browed, violent, someone indeed who was just himself in giant form.

To him this was a country rich with colour, and, accustomed to the biting, penetrating cold of the sea, the slight change in atmosphere as he walked inland was emphasized. What amazed him most were the trees that peopled it, some of enormous red-barked girth, others slender and silver boled, some spreading their branches as though they would fain cover the world, and others so lofty one's eyes watered gazing up at them. At Stonemerns there were hardly any trees and those few were dwarfed and twisted.

The autumn brightness made everything stand out curiously apart, everything seemed almost too clear, unreal. The trees looked rootless. The limes and planes were a dazzling yellow. The far-off mountains were blue with distance, the less remote lined with burns and broken into crags and patches.

He walked until it was night, gazing up at the full moon with its misty nebula and at the white clouds piled like snow. Annie had given him money and told him to ask a crofter for a bed, but Callum stopped at no thatched croft. He did not feel tired, but as it grew later he felt uneasily Annie would be expecting him to be in bed, so he chose out the biggest farm he could see. The moonshine made its collection of slated roofs look as though they were glistening with rain. He told the farmer he was walking to his work at Gilhead and asked if he would let him sleep in one of his outhouses. He spoke with pretended diffidence and tentatively offered him one of Annie's fourpenny bits. The man looked down at his cracked brogues and dusty clothes, then nodded brusquely in the direction of the loft, which was reached by a broken-down ladder. "Ye can bide there for the nicht," he said, "and ye can keep your money." It was on the tip of his tongue to add, "Ye look as though ye would need it a'," but instead he called out, "Ye can gang into the kitchen if ye like and tell them I sent ye ben for something to eat."

Callum did go into the kitchen, for it was not his way to reject anything he received for nothing, and after a plain but substantial meal he climbed into the loft. Its silence was only disturbed by his own movement amongst the hay and by the scampering and squeaking of innumerable rats. The moon shone in through the narrow, unglazed slits which served for windows and ventilation. Palely it lit up the tumbled hay in limited streaks, leaving the rest in a sea of obscurity. It silvered the enormous cobwebs which hung from the heavy rafters but it did not irradiate or penetrate to the back of the loft where large sacks of meal stood like burly peasant soldiers. Callum slept, and a full, ever waxing, yellow moon chased itself round and round his head. He awoke in the early morning with his nostrils filled with stour.

He arrived at Gilhead that night. The buoyancy he had felt on the previous day had deserted him. The air no longer stimulated him like wine, his feet no longer ate up the miles but dragged painfully. No longer did he feel the world was not big enough for him to walk round. It seemed a very vast and empty place with a trailing road whose end he could never hope to reach. He was no longer elated at the thought of a big farm and his new life. He wanted Annie—Annie and the familiarity of the stone kitchen with the window-panes keeping out the dark which was now closing down on him.

When he arrived at Inchbuigh Farm he wandered amongst the outhouses looking for the farm door, so drearily tired that he walked round them again and again. Then he heard voices. He stood quite still and listened. They were coming from behind a shut doors and they were talking Gaelic, but it was so different from the Gaelic spoken at Stonemerns that it might have been a foreign language. The voices also were different, not so flat but softer, with a sing-song inflection.

As he listened to those murmuring voices, Callum was conscious of a feeling which was to grow upon him as the years passed. Although he was in the world he felt cut off from it, as if he were there only on sufferance. To-night this feeling made him abjectly forlorn; as he grew older he felt desperately he would force his way through anything, stop at nothing, to break down this indefinable barrier, become one of its people, feel as they did ...

He did not take long to fit into his place, for the work came instinctively to him as though he had done it long ago and now all he needed was to grow accustomed to it again. When a whole litter of pigs died it was he who discovered their beds had been made with bracken, but no one had ever told him bracken was poisonous to pigs. When he found some sheep on the hills had their marked ears cut off, he knew to warn Robert Stewart there were "thieves' sheep up yonder". The smell of sheeps' wool at a shearing raised him to a peak almost of sublimity and the smell of milk warm from the cows struck gratefully on his nostrils, brought with it a wealth of comfort, made him remember that the cows were safe in their byres, the milk in its gIant cans.

He rose each morning at four o'clock and creaked downstairs to find his "piece" laid out for him on the dresser. He would steal across the silent bothy, unfamiliar because it was not full of movement and voices and the flickering of flames. Once outside the air that met him would be cuttingly cold and turn his large hands quite blue. He would go into the long byres and unchain the cows and goat, then drive them before him to the hills, the mist-damped grasses wetting his hardened, bare feet. He learnt to read the sun as one reads a clock and at nine, two and eight he brought the herd back to be milked.

On his way to and from the hills, he had to pass a piece of waste Iand where he always imagined a battle had been fought, perhaps because of the great ant-heaps which reminded him of mounded graves. Also the trees were stunted and stricken as though they grew up from earth veined with blood and drew their roots from wide-socketed skulls. It was called Cloutie's Croft and had never been sown or ploughed, for when the community was being formed this place had been left as a sanctuary for the spirits of trees to flee to when the woods and forests were cut down.

Another relic of ancient days was the knoll of trees in front of Inchbuigh Farm which had been the judgment ground. The three trees that had served as gallows were still standing, their branches overhanging a now crumbled dyke from which the condemned used to be pushed. Callum did not like passing this place at night in case the hungry spirit of some doomed robber still lurked there. He was afraid not of things but of the shadows that they threw; a curse would have haunted him more than any evil act he himself had perpetrated.

His duties did not end at being herd. Sometimes Robert or Ian Stewart would tell him to wash his feet. Then he would be made to stamp on barley, and oatmeal to pack them as tightly as possible into the chests. The barley-meal was not so bad but stamping on the oatmeal was like stamping on ice. Somehow he dreaded this duty more than any other, and it was not because the oatmeal was so cold ...

He liked best, when the cows were brought back at eight, to be told to fetch a basket or barrel and to go and help Miss Stewart pick the fruit in the garden. This garden had a peculiar fascination for him. It was apart from the dwelling and outhouses and was enclosed by a faced wall. There was a ghostliness about it even on the brightest day. It was so very old, the ground had been tilled and sown for so many hundreds of years that now the soil was as though drained. The flowers did not flame and bloom as in other gardens; they seemed wan, a little colourless. Despite its southern exposure and high, shielding walls, it lay grey and cold, a place of spent passion.

When Miss Stewart churned, Callum stood beside her and stroked the rich yellow butter with a knife to catch any hairs from the sieve. She was a robust woman with a kind enough heart but an acrid tongue and unprepossessing, acidulated manner. Her three brothers' wives were dead and lay in the graveyard amongst their husbands' kin, so she was mistress of the farm, but even when all her sisters-in-law had been alive she had still contrived to rule.

Callum was only allowed into the farm-house twice a week when he scrubbed out all the floors, while one of the servant girls followed him, drying as fast as he could scrub.

One day Ian Stewart presented him with a kilt. Callum was proud and gratified, particularly when he was told to wear it every day and not to keep it good for the Sabbath. It was not long, however, before he realized he had been given it so that he would wear out his knees and not his clothes. His temperament had always been suspicious and this discovery shook for all time his frail confidence in the humanity of man. A few days later, when Miss Stewart gave him an apple, he looked to see if it were bad.

Four times a year he was allowed to stop herding and young Fiona Stewart drove the cattle before her, whooping as she went. These were on the market days which fell in March, June, July and November. Callum would go with the other farm servants to Larch, some distance away, but, unlike them, he never went near the market. Instead he stood outside the inn and held the horses' heads. He liked when the farmers came out drunk for in that condition they could so easily mistake half a crown or a crown piece for a penny. Nine out of ten came out of the inn drunk. On market days they allowed themselves unwonted licence; also the innkeeper knew well how to stimulate an already whetted thirst, for always on his bar were plates with slices of salted mutton which were given to his patrons free of charge.

Callum had a morbid interest in drunken men. He believed in letting sleeping thoughts lie and could not understand why they should want to quicken their brains with drink. It would have brought no consolation to him, for his brain was charged all the time as though it were perpetually inflamed by some strong, unknown wine. It was not that his fermented thoughts moved excitedly, but his mind was a dark inn into which his thoughts entered like uninvited guests come to seek refuge from the storm. They sat round his inhospitable board and their voices held the melancholy of those who are accustomed to living by themselves. He would never dared get drunk, for he knew what came into his mind when conscious but no one could tell what would come if he were not there, watching ...

Most of his life for the next few years was spent on the lonely hill-side while his herd grazed scattered round him. Thunderstorms would pass below him and, dry as a bone, he would watch them from far above, feeling violently sick. The kindly sun would glance on the sullen hill-tops, and the strewn boulders, polished by rain, would shine and glisten. The distant fields round Inchbuigh Farm would become white with staring marguerites or yellow with wheat. Heavy, slanting showers of autumn rain would fall. The light green of the bracken would wither. Ghostly mists would steal down, silent and cold. Ice would form in the cart ruts and, as he drove them home, the cows' laboured breaths would sound like blowing bellows.

So the days passed into seasons and the seasons counted off years. From his far hill-top Callum still looked down on the infinitesimal whitewashed cottages and, behind a clump of trees, on Stewart's Farm with its haystacks and clustered outhouses and its fertile fields. He would watch a tiny shepherd and his fly of a dog crawling up a hill-side until he lost them in a gully. He would see the white dot of an aproned woman hanging up more white dots on an invisible thread. He would watch intently toiling pigmies of men with toy horses ploughing and tilling small squares of brown earth.

And sometimes as he sat there unbidden and most unallowable thoughts would form in his head. Why should he be herd? Why should he have to say nought to Howard Stewart when he called out at him? Why could he not give him the good clout he longed to give him? Why should he be sent to trudge miles to fetch water from an iron stream in the mountains for ailing young John? If he were ailing would anyone trudge a step for him?

Chapter Three

INCHBUIGH Farm was owned by three brothers, Donald, Robert and Ian Stewart. Robert was upright, vigorous and incisive, Ian had stooping shoulders and a Semitic cast of face. Everything they did prospered, but the star of Donald, the eldest, had never been in the ascendant. His two brothers had strong young sons to keep the farm going; he had only one child, a daughter, whose mother had died at her birth. He was so kind that when he had been herd as a boy he had always let the cows eat their way home instead of hurrying them to be back in time for his supper. People went to him when they were in trouble although he never did anything beyond be gentle, but there was something monumental in his fumbling, shambling presence. But he had never been of any use about the farm. He was undecided, slow on the uptake, not even "handy" with his fingers, and he had a maddening habit of never believing the worst even though it was staring him in the face. When the crops were ruined beyond all hope, he would say thoughtfully, "Mebbe, Ian, it will no be as bad as ye fear." This characteristic of his brother adversely influenced Ian who, as though to balance the scale, was gloomy and pessimistic, going out of his way to meet trouble more than half way.

Although Donald was the eldest, he occupied "the bothy," a building attached to the barns, while his brothers, with their families and sister, lived in the large farm-house. Every fine evening the old farmer sat on a seat at the gable end of the bothy and smoked his pipe, hailing impartially all those who passed. The seat was broken down, but he was now so used to the discomfort that each time he went over to have "a claver" with old Mistress Turner he wondered what was the matter with her seat. During the day he stood at the bothy door prophesying, always incorrectly, about the weather; or he would sit at the fire, his mouth fallen open while meditatively he felt his top gum with the extreme tip of his tongue. He possessed only two teeth which stood, yellow sentinels, in an otherwise deserted bottom gum. He supped in solitary state at a big table while the numerous farm hands had their meals crowded round a smaller one. He took sugar with his boiled egg instead of salt and the procedure by which he ate his porridge fascinated Callum. Two bowls were placed in front of him, one full of hot porridge, the other of cold milk, and he dipped his horn spoon by turns into each.

Callum shared a slit of a room with the ploughman in the bothy where he also had his meals, but very little of his time was spent indoors except to sleep. Sometimes, however, before going to bed he would sit on the high-backed settle for quarter of an hour to warm himself at the fire. He sat so quiet and still people forgot he was there. He would watch tentative Donald Stewart or the business-like Robert or Ian of the shifty smile. Their sons would pass the door or move in and out of the bothy shadows. Nothing that happened was missed by two black eyes under a sombre brow. He would watch Lizzie MacPhee, the milking-girl, look round sharply when Joe's tread crossed the yard although she would never turn when Howard or Sam or Tom entered. He would see Robert and Ian exchange glances over their brother's bent head, and he would watch Fiona cutting slices from a homemade loaf as though she were sawing the trunk of a tree.

She was Donald's only child, and the one pretty thing about her was her name. She was a stalwart little girl with roughened face and hands. Even in summer she always looked cold and her stunted nose was red as a rowan. She stumped more than walked and laughed instead of smiled, widely revealing blunt, square teeth. Her hair was a bright and ugly red, belying one's first impression of genial good nature. When she grew angry, which was not infrequently,she jumped from one foot to the other. Her conversation was peculiar, for it was punctuated with broken ejaculations which often had nothing to do with what she was saying, as though she were communing with herself at the same time as she was talking.

Callum liked to watch her, for everything she did was characteristic, from the way she set the table by bumping the articles on to it, to the very way she tied a knot.

But he had never exchanged more than a few words at a time with her until one evening when he was returning by the banks of the burn from a sheep-shearing. He was carrying his jacket, for although it was evening the day had been broiling and he felt so hot he was quite sure he would never know what it was to be cool again. When he turned a bend he nearly tripped over someone who was lying full length on her stomach on the bank.

It was Fiona Stewart, and she explained to him that she was guddling for trout. In her comradely way she invited him to come and have a guddle with her. He knew he had been sent back early from the sheep-shearing to help at the farm, but somehow the short-handed farm did not seem so important as this green, overhanging bank. Running water was surely the coolest sound on earth.

He lay down beside her and plunged his hands up to the elbows into the icy-cold burn.

"Wha throws the first trout oot will be marrit first. Hey, Callum Lamont!"she said.

He looked at her obliquely as she lay beside him. Her fiery hair dangled over her face and curtained it from his view. He looked at her curiously as though seeing her for the first time.

Suddenly she raised herself, her hair was flung over her shoulders and her arms moved like frantic windmill wheels as she threw something over her head. She turned to see the size of trout she had caught, her lips half parted to exclaim. Then he saw her face stiffen as though frozen. He never forgot the expression of loathing which crossed it as she drew herself perilously near the edge of the bank, like an animal expecting to be attacked.

His eyes followed her horrified stare and he saw that it was no trout she had caught but a rat, which was swiftly disappearing amongst the tall grasses.

"It willna touch ye," he said almost contemptuously, amazed to see she was shaking.

"I feel," she cried passionately, "as if ma haunds would ne'er get clean agin."

He did not know what prompted him to do it, indeed he did not realize what had happened until after it was done. He knelt forward on the bank, pushed her hair from her face, and roughly kissed her lips. Then, astounded, he looked at her to see her gazing back at him with startled, questioning eyes.

"Whit did ye do that for? Ho!" she said, and her voice wheezed. "I dinna ken," he answered, glowering darkly at her. "We'll have anither guddle."

But Fiona was never good at guddling after that, for every time she felt something touch her hands under the water they twitched involuntarily before they grasped and so she lost all her catches.

Callum began to think of her a great deal. His lips would tingle once more as they had tingled after he had kissed her, and he longed to feel again the coldness of her nose against his cheek. When he met her she would greet him with, "Ha, Callum Lamont!" and she would laugh to him, but he could never catch her eyes dwelling on him as he had sometimes seen them do before.

As he grew older he gained more confidence. There came stolen, memorable moments when he would kiss her in the hayloft or in the byre or when she would meet him with his herd. Those moments were always secret and apprehensive, except on the hill-side, where they were sure of being alone. In later years the smell of hay or warm milk or wild thyme would bring her back to him in a flood of remembrance which would take his breath away. His memory of her never shrank to any dim being, she never became comfortingly ghostly. When he had to think of her, she stepped from the very back of his mind as complete, as vigorous, as alive, as she had been when she had stood beside him.

He liked her presence, vaguely it satisfied him. She was one of the few people who did not make him writhe with a sense of unjust inferiority. She stimulated and made him feel powerful. He felt safe beside her. As a rowan tree guards a grave from evil spirits, so her presence warded from him unhappy things and dark thoughts.

He loved her with a love that was painful unless she was there to comfort him with her nearness. She stirred and satisfied him while she frustrated and maddened him. His caresses grew fiercer, more bites than kisses. She came very rarely to the hill-side for it was seldom she was able to get away from the farm, although often, he told himself morosely, she could have got away had she wanted. He would lie on the hill-side thinking of her until his longing became a lust. Her kisses were no longer sufficient for him and he hated her resoluteness, which was a wall between them he could not kiss through or pull down with threats and contentions.

He had always meant to leave Stewart's employment when he was seventeen or eighteen and find better work to do, in a city somewhere. But he was nineteen now and still herd at Inchbuigh Farm with only the prospects of becoming a ploughman. And the one thing that tethered him to Gilhead was a sturdy, wide-mouthed girl. He swore over and over again to himself that she was nothing to him, that he would leave the following month, but the following month still found him there, fuming at his own weakness.

One afternoon in early autumn he lay with his hands behind his head, glaring at a mossy stone, when he heard her footsteps on the turf. But he was sullen because it was so long since she had come to the hill-side, and pretended not to hear her. He did not move even when she stood looking down on him.

"Och-hey!" she said, sitting beside him, "I hurried on wi' the baking and so here I am."

He made no response.

"If ye're no going to ope your gab—huh," she pursued after a pause, "I'll be for getting awa'."

"Ye'll bide whaur ye are noo that ye are here," he said furiously, and he put his arm round her to keep her, for she had a disconcerting, unfeminine habit of doing what she said.

"Whit's the guid o' biding wi' ye if ye'll no speak?" she demanded.

"It's ye that's a' wrang," he replied, his voice muffled with wrath. "Ye could get awa' every day if ye hurried on wi' the baking."

"Ho! could I?" she retorted. "Ye would expect the sun to stop rising and the floors to stop growing because o' ye, Callum Lamont. I canna get awa'—ye ken that weel enow. But we're thegither noo—let's mak' the maist o' it," and she pulled his big head by the hair towards her.

"I'm going to get oot o' here," he said hoarsely.

"Ay," she acquiesced placidly, "the work's no guid enow for ye."

"Na, it isna," he returned, "and I'm no going to bide juist because ye think ye can play wi' me like a cat wi' a mouse."

"Ye're a fine hefty mouse, hey!" she said scornfully. "Ye can get awa' frae the cat when ye want to."

"I ken that," he replied dourly, "and this time next month ye can come to the hill-side at midnicht if ye want, but ye'll no find me a-waiting on ye."

She lay safely beside him in the crook of his arm, gazing up at him from between half-closed lids and colourless lashes while she ran her short fingers through his black hair.

In spite of himself he was pacified, as he always was, by her immediate presence. He stared down at the scattered clachan so far below them. She belonged to this country and at least a part of it belonged to her, for she was Donald's only child and Donald was the eldest of the three brothers.

"Your crops are graund and big this year," he said.

"It's no a guid sign when they are as heavy as a' that," she replied. "Aunt Myra wis for saying she had ne'er seen them so guid syne the year Graundfaether died a' of a sudden-like."

"I wish," Callum cried, suddenly passionate, "I had a farm a' to masel' wi' crops as heavy as gold."

"Weel, mebbe ye will have one o' them days."

"Michty near I'm getting to it herding anither man's cattle."

"Huh! ye ken weel enow, Callum Lamont, that if ye had one farm it would no be lang afore ye would be casting your een on your neebour's."

"One would be enow to be going on wi'. Ye folk—ye've got everything."

"I would no say that," she answered slowly.

"It's no oor farm—only in a kind o' a way— we juist tenant it frae the Marquis o' More-neck."

"I thocht it belanged to ye," he said, startled. "I thocht ye had farmed there for years and years."

"Ay, and so we have. A Stewart's had Inchbuigh lang afore the Morenecks were heard o', and we used to own it, but we were done oot o' it by a Marquis near twa hundred year back. He wis oot riding one day and meets Stewart on the high-road and stops to speak to him. He gets their talk roond to title-deeds and such-like. 'I believe your title-deeds are the auldest in the shire,' he said to him, and asks him to bring them up to the Castle next day so that he could compare them wi' his ain. Up gangs Stewart to the Castle wi' his title-deeds, in comes the Marquis and tak's them awa', saying his ain are in the next room. Stewart waited and waited and waited until e'en he grows uneasy. He opens a door and creeps to a servant, wha tellt him it was time he was getting hame noo, and that was the last he e'er saw o' his title-deeds."

"He micht have kent whit would happen," Callum said bitterly. "I would ken no man would stop on a horse and talk to me unless he wantit something."

"Ay," she agreed, "when ye're such a fool as a' that ye maun expect to be fooled. But he was a hard, bad man, yon Marquis, and did mair than us oot o' oor due. A MacNab used to own Murthole that the Disharts tenant now. The Marquis had a small thirlage on it and twice a year MacNab rode to Edinburgh to get the money to pay the interest on it. One nicht aifter he had been he cam' hame so tired he juist took aff his boots and went to his bed. The next morning he rode to the Castle wi' the money, but the Marquis would no tak' it frae him for he was a day late wi' it. He shut up the thirlage and MacNab had to tenant the farm he used to own. It's always been an ill-boded place, yon Murthole—they say thirled places always are."

"Whit is the Marquis like noo?" he inquired.

"Huh, he'll ne'er do whit he promises—he'll say onything except his prayers. But the Marchioness is a guid women, although they say she's mair like a man to look at than a woman, wi' a stride on her like a horse. But we have naething to do wi' them; they have their castles and can spare us oor farm."

Callum gazed down at where the bland farm-house was hidden behind a clump of trees, and his heart stirred within him. He had very patriarchal ideas. He would have liked a farm of his own with well-filled outhouses and flourishing crops and men to order about. He would have liked seven sons all over six feet, except perhaps the youngest ...

Chapter Four

IT was some time later, one night in October, that Callum was awakened by loud voices in the next room where Donald Stewart slept. He was often disturbed at night by hearing the old man calling out in his sleep, for he had bad nightmares that a bull was chasing him and that he, being infirm and stiff now, could not escape from it.

To-night, however, it was not one clamouring voice Callum heard but several which were raised as though in altercation. He lay still for some minutes, drowsily trying to disentangle them, when certain words, striking upon his newly-awakened ears, made him sit up in bed to listen more attentively.

"Weel," Robert Stewart's incisive voice had said, "if they're no turning us oot, whit are they telling us to gang for?"

"It canna be, it canna be," reiterated Donald, whose brain was still fogged with the heavy sleep of the very old or the very weary. "We canna leave Inchbuigh—there's nowhere else to gang to."

"That's naething to the Marquis o' Moreneck," said Jan. His voice was easily distinguishable from the others for it was hoarse, as though at the back of his throat there hung a curtain of phlegm which blew in and out with his breath.

"He disna want us," sneered Joe, Robert's eldest son, "sheep will pay him mair."

"It's an ill thing," came Donald's slow voice again, "to turn men and women and bairns oot o' their hames for sheep."

"If ill things pay the Marquis o' Moreneck," rasped Ian, "he'll no stop short at doing them."

"It canna be, it canna be," said Donald, and his voice almost pled with them to reassure him." We've had Inchbuigh a' them years, the farm's as guid as oors. We've paid its worth in rent o'er and o'er and o'er agin."

"Ye ne'er believe the worst, Donald Stewart," said Ian, "and so it always finds ye unprepared. Mind whit happened in Sutherland and whit's happening in Ross-shire noo. The commissioner didna say a' yon to Joe juist for the sake o' hearing his ain voice."

"Whit was it he said, whit was it?" asked Donald. "Ye cam' in upon me so quick…"

"Weel," came Joe's sullen tones, "I gangs into Mr. Geddes and pays him the rent. 'Oh, Mr. Stewart,' says he to me, as though he had juist minded something a' of a sudden-like, 'this is the last rent I expect to have frae ye.' 'Is it?' says I, thinking he's cracking a joke though he's no a joking man. 'And hoo can that be, Mr. Geddes?' asks I. 'No rent is to be demanded in May,' says he, 'for the districts Gilhead and Larch are to be laid under sheep. Ye micht be so guid as to tell your neebours.' I was so dumbfoundered I juist looks at him, but he looks everywhaur but at me wi' his wicked wee een like a goat. Then I says, 'Mr. Geddes, I'll tell ma neebours no such thing. The Marquis can get men like ye to do his bloody work but he'll no get me'."

"Ye should no have said yon noo, Joe," reproved his Uncle Donald. "There's no guid making an enemy."

"I said mair to him than yon," answered Joe, his voice rising.

"Muckle guid it will do us," muttered Howard, Ian's son.

"And whit would ye have done?" jeered Joe. "Sucked it a' in like an unweaned lamb?"

"Ye did richt enow, Joe," said his father. "It's mair than flesh and blood can staund. The thing noo is to decide whit we are to do aboot it."

"The best thing to do," Donald said momentously, "is for us to see Mr. Cameron. He's a guid man and will guide us——"

"It's no a meenister we need," put in Joe, "it's a regiment o' sodgers."

"Violence begets violence," rebuked Donald.

"I'll ride to Edinburgh the morn's morn and see Mr. Scrivener," Ian said uneasily. "He'll ken the ins and oots o' it a' and will ken if they can do it, but I doot, I doot, I verra much doot …"

Callum listened to their footsteps stumbling down the uneven bothy stairs. He sat quite motionless, gazing into the dark. The ploughman beside him had slept through it all. He lay on his back, his mouth wide open, and snored lustily like a snorting pig.

Suddenly Callum felt the room stiflingly hot. He rose and pushed open the creaking skylight, standing on his square toes to reach the ladlelike handle. The sound of the burn came in with a rush—the burn which made the coolest sound on earth, which watered the desolate Pass of Naver and coursed its precipitous way through Gilhead and Larch. He shoved a block of wood between the skylight and the frame to keep it open.

The bothy was very still. Something made him cross the floor, lift the latch of his door and steal out on to the landing. Donald Stewart's door was ajar and he peeped into the room. The old man was still sitting up in bed, grabbing at the blankets as though for support. He looked like some propped-up, grotesque effigy in his flannel nightshirt. Callum, as he peered in at him, suddenly thought of that other Stewart who had so amiably taken his invaluable title-deeds to the Marquis of Moreneck.

For the first time that he could remember the morning took a long time to come. He lay awake waiting for it. Duiguid disgusted him with his animal snores, which seemed to shake the whole room. His mouth was like the opening in the spout of a kettle, with his underlip projecting farther than his upper. He rose at four, shivering with cold, and as he unchained the cows he wondered if they knew what had happened. In the greying morning light they looked ghostly, and as he drove them, lowing, before him they seemed to huddle together.

The atmosphere was disturbed and troubled. Callum would be told to go into the farmhouse kitchen for his porridge because Dishart, from Murthole, would be talking to Donald and his brothers in the bothy behind a closed door. Sometimes in the evening grave-faced crofters would come in small bands of twos and threes. Ian Stewart came back from Edinburgh, and after his return the gloom was intensified. The air became heavy with a pall of foreboding, whisperings and half-voiced doubts.

Nothing was discussed freely until the summonses of ejection were delivered impartially to the humblest crofter and the most prosperous farmer. Until then most of the crofters had taken the warning reverberations like Donald and preferred not to believe them, but now they could no longer shut their eyes to what was to happen.

On the day the summonses were received Fiona told Callum that a meeting was to be held that night in the bothy kitchen.

She had his supper ready for him as usual, for the crofters were not expected until after nine o'clock. When he was finishing Joe Stewart entered and leant against the high mantelshelf. He was a big, silent man with a bad-humoured, handsome face which was now darkly clouded as though he saw something dire happening before his very eyes.

Callum pushed back his chair from the table and prepared to go upstairs to bed, but as he passed behind the tall back of the settle he paused. The settle was old-fashioned and heavily built; at the back there hung a flap of wood which, when lifted, revealed a cupboard where firewood was kept. The hollow was large enough to hold a man if he bent almost double amongst the crackling twigs.

Callum had pushed open the door in order to go upstairs. It creaked back on its unoiled hinges, but he was neither on the outside nor the inside. It was as though an invisible agency had swallowed him.

The crofters came in severally, greeting Donald deferentially and Joe with more familiarity. Two or three shepherds with their dogs were the first to arrive. They all, except Joe, tried manfully to keep the conversation afloat.

"That looks a fine crushie ye have, MacAlpine," said Donald.

"Ay, it's been a guid dog to me," answered MacAlpine in a voice surprisingly falsetto coming from so massive a man. "It's got the Gaelic but no the English."

"Sensible crushie," Joe said harshly.

"Crushies are queer stock," said another man in order to break an awkward pause. "I've heard tell o' them turning on shepherds wha have had them for years and sometimes worrying them to deith."

"Aweel," MacAlpine returned leniently, "I dinna think a crushie likes to see his masiter growing auld."

The tread of booted feet was heard and the bothy shook as more crofters crossed the floor. About twenty congregated in the kitchen. Conversation was scanty and painful while they fidgeted in their wooden seats and repeatedly cleared their throats, until Robert Stewart entered with Ian and Howard behind him.

"Guid evening a'," he said, characteristically brisk. "Are we a' here?"

"Na, Mr. Cameron's no," said Taggart, an elder. He was large pored like an orange and he sat on the very edge of his chair as though to be on the alert to contradict any misstatements.

"Faether cudna come, he has the rheumatics that bad," piped up young MacPherson, "but he said I wis to say to ye that whate'er Mr. Donald Stewart said he would staund to."

A quick, light footstep was heard and the black silhouette of a thin, high-shouldered man stood in the bothy doorway. When he entered the kitchen, chairs were scraped back and there was a general commotion as the heavy-bodied crofters stood. A clipped voice, different from the others in timbre and accent, wished them all good-evening. There was a long, expectant pause when everyone was once more seated. It was broken at last by Joe.

"Weel, Mr. Cameron, and whit in your opeenion is the best thing we should do?" He spoke aggressively, as if the subject had been discussed before, and not amicably, between him and Mr. Cameron.

"I have told you already that you can do nothing," pronounced the minister. He leant forward with both hands on the knob of his stick and his pointed face nodded at the fire.

"That's a hard thing to say, Mr. Cameron," said Robert Stewart.

"It's men and women being driven frae their names, no cattle being herded oot o' sheds," MacPhee, the molecatcher, put in excitedly.

"We must all, from the lowest to the highest, learn to accept what God sees fit to send us," the minister said deliberately. "Besides," he added a minute later, "you have been given fair warning."

"We've been gi'en legal warning," said Dishart of Murthole, "but things that are legal are no always fair."

"God's law speaks through the heart," sighed Donald Stewart, "and legal law is written wi' the haund."

"Let each one of us," continued the minister, "try to see His Finger working even in misfortune for our benefit."

"I dinna see whit benefit can come oot o' hameless men and women wi' their bairns," muttered Howard Stewart.

"This may be a fitting punishment sent from on high for our unchastened secret pride," the minister said severely.

"Then, Mr. Cameron," came a stentorian voice which made them all jump, for it seemed startlingly to come from nowhere, "by your way o' it the Marquis o' Moreneck is inspired by God and no by sheep."

There was a moment of appalled silence as everyone gazed round to see whom it was who had spoken, but their attention was arrested again by Joe, who seized on the words of the unseen speaker.

"Ay, ay," he thundered, feeling the words were full of strength, "is the Marquis inspired by God or by sheep, Mr. Cameron?"

"For shame, for shame, Joe Stewart, so wantonly bringing your Maker's Name into a wordly argument," cried the minister.

There was another long pause which was broken by the voice, now low and ingratiating.

"If the Finger o' God is to be foond in badness, Mr. Cameron, whit is the guid o' being guid and law-abiding?"

"Ay, ay," cried Joe, "whit is the guid?"

"My Lord Marquis," vindicated the minister, raising his voice, "has rented us these crofts and farms for years out of the kindness of his heart."

"We've been peaceable tenants to him," remarked Robert Stewart, "and farmed his lands weel."

"We spilt oor best blood in the past to keep him his lands," said Crearar.

"I lost ma twa sons at Waterloo," said MacNaughton, lifting up an old and wrinkled face.

"These lands belong to his Lordship," went on the minister, "and they are his to do what he likes with. If he wants them now, it is right he should have them. We must remember we are as nothing to one who is as high as my Lord Marquis."

"And my Lord Marquis," declaimed the bodyless, shouting voice, "will be juist as sma' as ony o' us on the Judgment Day."

There was general consternation at this declaration. The minister stood up and, facing the wag at the wa' clock, cried out:

"Who dares to speak like this?"

Only empty silence received his question, a silence which became burdened with tiny creakings and sighing breaths as the crofters, hardly daring to look over their shoulders, waited for something to happen. The bothy kitchen had three doors leading from it, a hole in the wall for peat, a hole in the roof to a loft, and a gaping, cavernous chimney. It was all these apertures which made the reverberating voice sound each time it spoke as though coming from a different place.

Martin, the carter, who was practically stone deaf, suddenly said urgently :

"Time disna sleep, ye ken. Time's getting on, ye ken. May's coming nearer and nearer every meenit, ye ken, and we maun think whit we are to do."

The other crofters knocked their thick sticks on the floor to show their approval.

"Ay," MacNaughton assented slowly, "whit are we to do and whaur are we to gang?"

Everyone looked out of the corners of his eyes towards Mr. Cameron, but he remained thin-lipped, mute and motionless. Then the voice came again, muffled but authoritative, and now it sounded as though it were coming from below the table.

"I tell ye whit to do," it said. "Whit ye need is a spokesman— someone wha can talk the English as weel as he can talk the Gaelic. Mr. Cameron will do. Get him to ride to the Marquis o' Moreneck, get him to tell him if Gilhead and Larch are laid under sheep, o'er one thousand men, women and bairns will have no hames. Get Mr. Cameron to ask the Marquis whit he is to do wi' his congregation when they are driven frae their work and hames. And if the Marquis will no see Mr. Cameron, get Mr. Cameron to see the Marchioness. She'll no turn a deaf ear." There were murmurs of assent.

"If Mr. Cameron disna get or canna force himsel' into the Castle," pursued the voice, "get Mr. Cameron to gang to Edinburgh and stir up publeec opeenion aboot it. A guid way to do it," it added more faintly but reflectively, "would be to begin and raise funds for the ejected."

"I go to the Marquis?" cried the minister, springing to his feet again. "I will do no such thing."

"Why no?" interrogated the voice.

"I—go—to—the—Marquis?" repeated Mr. Cameron, as though unable to believe what he was saying. "I dare do no such thing."

"Why no?" insisted the voice.

"I couldn't move him," argued the minister, "I would have no effect upon him. He would never listen to such as me."

"Ye are in the habit o' the kirk," the voice continued inexorably, "and the Marquis o' Moreneck should listen to whit a meenister o' God has to say."

"Come out, come out, whoever you be," called Mr. Cameron, standing petrified in the middle of the floor and now blankly facing the doorway.

"Will ye gang or will ye no gang?" roared Joe Stewart.

"Go!" exclaimed the minister. "I will not go a step."

"Come, come, Mr. Cameron," said Dishart of Murthole, "it's no muckle to ask o' a guid man like ye. It's oor one chance and God will uphold ye."

"I could do no such thing," said the minister, who was shaking from head to foot.

"Are ye feart," the baleful voice insinuated, "that if ye gang ye'll mebbe lose the ither living the Marquis will find ye when the kirk at Larch is burnt doon for sheep?"

"Is it the deil you have tethered to your house, Mr. Stewart?" mouthed the minister.

"By God, I'll mak' ye gang then," said Joe, and his huge body lunged towards him.

"Joe, Joe, dinna strike a meenister," his Uncle Donald cried in terrified protest, half risen from his chair.

"No under your ain roof noo, Joe," his father said more tolerantly.

"Think shame on yoursel'," rebuked Taggart, the elder.

But Joe was beside himself.

"I'll ficht ye, I'll ficht ye," he shouted, "and if God is on your and the Marquis's side, He'll no forsake ye."

"Your soul is black, Joe Stewart, and only the pit awaits you," said the minister, standing high-shouldered and rigid in the doorway, and his tapering nose threw a shadow on his face like the shadow of the needle on a sundial. "Satan speaks through your mouth. You are in league with the deil, whom you can call up at will. It is not through the Marquis but through him that calamity has fallen on this farm and that your relatives have come to grief. Taggart and Christy and MacOuat, as elders of the kirk, I adjure you to leave a house that is cursed by the presence of Satan and never to enter it again."

Chapter Five

AFTER some weeks of deliberation and thought the crofters determined to send a deputation to the Marquis. Accordingly lots were drawn and fell to, amongst others, two shepherds, young MacPhee, the mole-catcher's open-mouthed son, and old Martin, who was practically stone deaf. It was as though a malicious fate had chosen from their midst the eight most ineffectual.

A week later they set out, clad in their Sabbath blacks, for Gel Castle, the seat of his Lordship. They were grimly nervous and ill at ease, but as they walked through the stricken clachans they gathered courage, for many more joined their band. Children ran out to cheer as they passed, women gave them food, and old men wished them God speed. Hearts beat quicker, blood rose higher, and the tramp of their feet became almost rhythmic, like the tramp of soldiers. Through the Pass of Naver, over the Fionn moors, ferried across Loch Tarrol, through Drura and Auchendee, past a shabby manse on the Loch's side, to little Barnfingal. Then, leaving the Loch, up a steep brae; now through Muccoth and over the wild, turfy hills.

The village of Gel is at last sighted, they come at last upon the Castle with its slender gates, whose intricate traceries glisten with rain, and which yield reluctantly. The black figures stream up the avenue. They stand, dumbly waiting for the doors to be opened, dwarfed by the pile of forbidding grey stone which makes their three score seem a mere scattering. The doors are opened. One man stands out from the rest and asks to see the Marquis. He is told regretfully that the Marquis and Marchioness left Gel only yesterday for London. They gaze at the closed doors like uncomprehending sheep, then slowly they turn and wind down the sweep of avenue, like mourners at a funeral, no longer like marching soldiers.

When the deputation returned to Gilhead a stupor seemed to settle on the inhabitants. Only now did they realize to the fullest what was to happen and, as children watch the sea creeping upon their castle of sand, so they waited powerless for May to come.

But always, at the very back of their minds, there lay the unformed hope to which they clung with desperation that something would happen, that it was so bad it could not possibly be true. It did not bear contemplating and it hurt them when Dishart left Murthole. It made it all seem so real when the big, gloomy, flat-faced house, blinded by trees, was abandoned.

Things were happening around them which were so incredible they only increased the feeling of stupor. Cattle and goats, produce and stock, were being sold for next to nothing at the glutted markets. The Stewarts were making arrangements. Old Donald and Miss Myra Stewart and young Fiona were to go to relatives in Canada. Tom, Joe, Howard, John and Sam were to be sent to the Lowlands to find work. Highland farmers were prosperous in their crops and stock, not in ready-money. No one knew what was to become of Robert and Ian.

When Fiona heard she was to go to Canada, the bottom seemed to fall out of the earth. She fled to the hill where Callum sat beside his herd and there they clung together as though the whole world were trying to separate them, but it was she who was the desperate one now. He held himself a little rigidly as the thought revolved round and round in his brain that if yon grey sea got atween them they micht as weel be deid to each other. He was startled that this prospect did not appal him more.

"Och-hey, och-hey," she was lamenting, "it's a' bad thegither that is happening. But ho! it will a' come back on them that causes it. If ye do bad things, they'll turn on ye in the end like crushies gone savage."

"If the Marquis o' Moreneck breaks his neck," he said roughly, "it's no keeping ye and me thegither, is it?"

"I ken that, I ken that. But, Callum, I'll no gang to Canada. I can gang into service until ye mak' enow to marry me. But mind ye this, Callum Lamont, I'm gi'eing up ma faether for ye. Och-hey, but I wunner if I am doing richt. And ye maun swear by a' ye haud sacred that ye'll be true to me."

"Ay, I'll swear onything ye like," he muttered.

He heard her telling him they were to sail for Canada in a sloop at the end of April. She told him that she dared not tell anyone she was not going. She stood on one foot and then on the other and said she would have to pretend she was going until the very end, when she would be missing. Once the sloop was safely away she would go to her uncles, wherever they happened to be, and tell them that she had missed it and so had best go into service now.

His mind strove desperately to find some flaw in so simple a scheme. He was no longer listening to what she was saying. Something within him, something apart which did not seem to belong to him, something over which he had no influence, was praying sicklily that she would be forced to go to Canada. Thoughts such as these made him uneasy, for he did not want to acknowledge them; it was as though they ran on farther than he intended them to do. But surely it was better to have her torn brutally from him for all time than they should be linked so irrevocably together her stalking fate could not distinguish them apart ...He still loved her, but he was frightened by her unhappiness, afraid with a superstitious dread that she would taint him with it. She was a rowan tree whose berries had withered and whose roots had dried, a charm that no longer worked, a totem turned tabu.

Before the end of April Donald Stewart had a stroke and became too ill to be moved. He lay in a half-comatose condition while the hours fretted away April and ate into May.

The fateful day arrived. At an early hour word was brought to Inchbuigh that the Fiscal and the factor had arrived at Naver, a tiny clachan at the head of the Pass. They evidently expected opposition, for they were escorted by a strong body of constables and sheriff-officers. Finding none of the cottages abandoned, they gave the inmates half an hour to pack and carry away their furniture, after which the cottages were to be set on fire.

All that morning there was a continual file down the glen of men and women and children, all carrying something and all with the white, doomed faces of refugees. It was twelve o'clock before the Fiscal and his company were sighted from Inchbuigh, and then a shepherd's cottage far up the glen was seen to be on fire. They seemed to move with alarming swiftness, for first one, then two, three, four cottages were alight. The thatch of the crofts lit and blazed with a pitiful rapidity. The people were bewildered in a dumb, stupefied way, like people suddenly deprived of all speech and movement; even the children hardly cried. It was as though they were waiting to awaken and find it all a dream.

With the inevitability of fate the fires advanced down the glen. Nothing deterred the Fiscal and his company in their purpose. Two children of MacAlpine, the shepherd, lay sick with a fever but were turned out on the moor while the cottage was burnt down. Old Widow Colquhoun refused to leave the only home she had ever known and the sheriff-officers had themselves to take her out forcibly when her blankets were on fire. The carter was made to carry his pregnant wife out of their cottage; while it burned she lay on a blanket outside and within an hour died.

They arrived at Inchbuigh between three and four o'clock in the afternoon. Ian Stewart stood out to speak to them.

"Guid aifternoon, Mr. Montrose," he said.

"Guid aifternoon to you, Mr. Stewart," the factor replied shortly.

"The farm's ready for ye," went on Ian, "but ye'll kindly leave the bothy. Ma brither's ill and canna be moved as mebbe ye have heard."

"We've got our orders, Mr. Stewart."

"Ay, Mr. Montrose, and ye'll carry them oot if I ken ye aricht and if it pays ye. But ye daurna touch the barns, for the grain we've no been able to sell is still there, and the bothy's on to the barns. If ye fire one ye'll have to fire them a'."

"You should have moved your brither ere this."

"I tell ye he's too ill to be moved."

"Well, he'll need to be moved now. They've moved out dying women, so——"

"Mair shame to ye, Mr. Montrose."

"You were no asked for your opinion, Mr. Stewart. I have my orders."

"Oor grain's still in the barns and I tell ye it's no legal to burn barns whaur a tenant's grain is still stored."

"And I tell you we have no the time to gang discussing legalities with you the now. You've had fair warning, but I'll give you half an hour longer to move out your brother afore we start on the barns."

For a second or two Ian Stewart stood, his eyes narrowed, as though undecided what to do. Then he rapped out orders to his men to carry the meal-chests to safety. The men worked like trojans, and while they were saving the grain the empty farm-house was set on fire. The smoke came between the slates in wicked little puffs, then part of the roof collapsed and the flames leapt up like devils.

The barns were lit next and the fire, with the wind acting as giant bellows, swept over them towards the bothy. Donald Stewart had been carried out to the yard, where he lay in a stupor. But now the roaring, crackling flames seemed to penetrate into his brain and wildly lighten up its dim corners. A cart, harnessed to two neighing horses, was brought into the yard and several men went forward to help him into it, but he half rose to his feet of his own accord and stumbled forward, his eyes staring.

"Robert! Ian! Whaur are ye?" he cried. "It's Inchbuigh that's burning."

"Ay," Ian's voice said behind him, "it's Inchbuigh that's burning, Donald. Ye mind ye ne'er would believe me."

"I tell ye, I tell ye, I tell ye," cried Donald, and his voice rose to a mad, shrill pipe, "they can do whit they like but I'll dee Stewart o' Inchbuigh."

He moved across the yard and before anyone could stop him he had tottered into the bright flames that were now devouring the bothy. They leapt, roaring, higher and higher, as though trying to reach something just beyond their yellow tongues. Howard and young John dashed in after him but both were beaten back by the flames.

What happened next was like a hideous nightmare to Callum. He never knew whether the soldiers were drunk or merely malicious, but before they left the ruined, flaming farmhouse and its steadings, they went to the top of the knoll where the meal-chests had been carried for safety. They rolled them down the hill and watched them smash to atoms at the foot while the grain flew out in dusty clouds.

For long into the night Callum stood on the bridge, leaning on his stick. The air was filled with an odious stench which came from the sooty rafters of burning cottages. It was a dark night, but every now and then the darkness would be suddenly cut and a shower of sparks and flames would spring up as the undermined gable of a cottage tottered.

They were gone in a day…those pleasant crofts with their whitewashed cottages whose thatched roofs had sheltered so many. Murthole, Torben, Inchbuigh…families scattered as the grain of the fey-crop had been scattered. Gone was the farm where he had worked, where Miss Stewart had ruled in her despotically kind way, the bothy with its low rafters and friendly shadows…All gone, all gone, all gone as though they had never been…And the garden, the grey garden…weeds, like palm trees, would choke it …Slowly he turned away and found the road which was to take him back to Stonemerns. The night was full of strange, unfamiliar sounds, of little whimpers and lagging footsteps and husky Gaelic whisperings. Figures loomed out of the dark and then faded back into it again.

For more than a week spiral columns of smoke could be seen coming from the charred ruins of the cottages. By that time the uncertain ghosts who had peopled the moors after the evictions had all been driven away. Many went to Canada in a ship so rotten they could pick the wood out of her sides with their fingers. Some died of smallpox and dysentery on the voyage and the survivors counted them fortunate, for by death they escaped the misery, the poverty and incredible hardship they had to endure. The young men filtered to the Lowlands, where they became weavers or worked in factories and were thought droll and stupid with their slow, gentle, country manners. But most of the families wandered to the sea shore. They drifted there in hordes until they blackened the narrow, stony beach. They lived on shell-fish and seaweed, and listened to the waves rolling on the dreary shore while they looked blankly out to sea, waiting and watching for the pointing finger of God.

Chapter Six

FIONA could milk cows before she was eight and make butter before she was ten, but in service she was like a bull in a china shop. Mistresses engaged her because she looked strong and a hard worker, but she lost many places, usually through rudeness. Certainly she was not the servant type, she thought, as she slapped the bread board on to the table. Farming blood ran through her veins, and although she could have managed a large farmhouse with ease, the routine of service tried, hampered and confined her. Somehow she never dreamt of trying to procure work on a farm; better to be an exile than a prisoner in one's own country. At first she thought, instead of becoming a kitchen servant, of being a nursemaid, but she did not like children. A big, sturdy baby of one's own would not be so bad, but other people's children, whom one could not even slap, were impossible.

So she went from place to place, slept in garrets and worked in basement kitchens, ate butter sold in the shops as "soiled butter for servants," washed greasy dishes and broke drawing-room ornaments because she dusted them with such vigour. She used to think she would die unless she got one more breath of mountain air, or smelt again the smell of wind through wet grasses. But she did not die. Five o'clock came round each morning, the procession of dirty dishes began all over again, and she had to tell herself grimly that evidently it took a lot to kill Fiona Stewart.

Things would be going ostensibly smoothly when suddenly she would flare up at nothing or not answer when addressed. She might be cooking beans at the time, and they were not to know that as the beans leapt in the boiling water they reminded her of little trout. Trout brought back a green, overhanging bank and the rippling sound of water flowing over stones, and a square, savage face full of black mystery. Ho! mind how he used to tickle the trout until they lay still? Och-hey, what did beans matter when there were little brown-spotted fish darting here and there in shallow, sun-mottled pools? God, to think that burn was still flowing down the Pass of Naver, through Larch and Gilhead ...

Situations became increasingly difficult to find. Prospective mistresses wrote to former mistresses for her "character" and accordingly were discouraged from engaging her. Those who were impressed by her obvious capabilities felt uneasily at the end of the interview that she had found out a great deal about them and that they had learnt very little about her.

Looking for work grew monotonous, finally anxious. Likely mistresses found her more amenable. To a Mrs. Mather she was even amiable, for Mrs. Mather lived in a small house, a big consideration to a general servant. The only drawback to the situation from Fiona's point of view was a sickly little boy with a bound-up head, but she learnt to her relief that he had neither brothers nor sisters.

Mrs. Mather always had great difficulty in making up her mind and she could not decide whether or not to engage Fiona. While she floundered in a morass of indecision and asked the same questions over and over again, she gazed at her with faded, troubled eyes as though beseeching her to make up her mind for her.

At last she went out of the room holding Robert's hand and murmuring she had to see about something. Fiona then heard her saying in lowered tones outside the door, "Bobbin darling, do help poor mamma. Do you like her?" "Better than Sarah Wilkie?" it continued anxiously. "You remember, dear, the tall thin one who came yesterday afternoon when you were playing with your soldiers?" Gaunt Sarah Wilkie had looked as though she certainly would not have lent Robert the rolling-pin, so his inaudible reply was in favour of Fiona. "Do you think," pursued the hurried, nervous voice, "that papa will consider I have done wisely?" Robert was not sure, but after some more whispered dialogue Mrs. Mather returned to Fiona and diffidently presented her with arles (engagement money).

On the whole Robert did not regret his choice, although the new servant would never allow him into the kitchen and stolidly refused to tidy away his toys for him when his mother was out. But she gave him haricot beans to play with and the creamy spoons to lick.

She was more mistress of the house than Mrs. Mather. It was she who determined what was to be for to-morrow's dinner, who confronted the grocer about an overcharge and discovered the milk was being watered. Mrs. Mather grew to depend upon her so much that, in spite of herself, she kept her. Once when a meal was late she very naturally went into the kitchen and remarked tentatively that Mr. Mather was waiting. She was obviously startled but pretended not to hear her maid's quick retort that he would just have to bide until she was ready. She considered tremulously for some days about dismissing her, but Robert's earache grew worse and it was Fiona who thought of heating all the dinner plates and applying them, hot and comforting, one after another, to the side of his throbbing face.

She cooked for them, washed, scrubbed, dusted, baked— did everything in fact but think for them, and perhaps, she thought rudely, they would be brighter if she did. It was their lifelessness which depressed her. Mr. Mather might have been an automatum wound up every night to go to his business next day, read his paper, execute his work and write his small cheques. What good was life—vital, unprocurable life—to Mrs. Mather, who fretted it away worrying ceaselessly over trivialities? Even the child Robert was listless, grew so quickly tired of his too-numerous playthings.

When the day's work was done Fiona would sit at the kitchen hearth, her knees spread out, the glow from the fire reddening her slapped-looking arms and deepening the fiery tints of her hair. She would think until she ached of a knoll of wind-blown trees, of green moss, like pincushions, studding a slated roof, of the cuckoo's spittle clinging to grasses that lay in the shadow of the dyke, of the grass-grown tops of black fanks. Her heart would thump unevenly at her side as she thought of a strange, watching face. Ho, to see him again standing so firmly beside her, to feel again the roughness of his kisses—Callum, who was so sure of himself, who would move the whole world to get what he wanted, who would free her from this serfdom ...her blessed Callum.

Chapter Seven

THERE was nothing welcoming in the familiarity of the flat, dreary moors. Callum's mood of gloom intensified as he walked across them towards the sea. He felt by returning to Stonemerns he had somehow slipped back. The forgotten stench of fish assailed his nostrils and filled him with a nauseating depression. The cottages were poorer, more huddled together and dilapidated than he had imagined; the Lamonts' looked chill, even uninviting.

When he reached the gusty corner where it stood the sound of the wind suddenly strung his heart. Long-ago, buried memories crowded upon him when he had lain in bed at night with darkness all around him. Then the world had seemed a vast void habited by only one small dwelling which stood insecurely on the edge of creeping moors. The sea had been a living thing, crumbling, fretting, gnawing the earth away to reach the cottage. But he had felt no terror of the creak-ridden darkness; instead he had been filled by a feeling of tense, almost breathless imminence.

Annie Lamont came out of the kitchen to see who could be entering the house instead of "chapping" on the door. He thought she was going to faint as her eyes stared back at him, first blankly, then with a certain desperation. The colour drained from her thin face and left it mottled with tiny purple, burst veins. She looked almost hunted as she backed into the kitchen before him.

"So, Callum," she said with difficulty, "it's ye."

"Ay," he answered shortly, "it's me."

He sat down on a chair and she watched him while she strove to gather her scattered thoughts together.

"Ye've got back," she said at last in her toneless voice.

"Ay," he replied, "I've got back."

Her eyes left him and wandered round the room until they fell on the fireplace.

"Mither's deid," she said.

"I ken that," he replied almost rebukingly. "Ye tellt me in a letter."

"Ye ne'er answered," she said, "so I wunnered if ye had left Inchbuigh and ne'er got them."

"Ay, I got them a' richt."

"That was why I stopped writing to ye," she said more loudly than it was her wont to speak.

She prepared a meal for him which he ate in accustomed silence. He never betrayed it, he did not admit it even to himself, but Annie's attitude had upset him. It was only too evident she was not pleased to see him, and this knowledge disturbed him. In those years that had passed there had always lain at the back of his mind the thought that if the worst did come to the worst he could return to Annie. And now Annie did not want him, stared at him with dilated, unbelieving eyes. Her letters to him had stopped some years ago. Apparently she had been quite content to think he had left Inchbuigh and that she would never see him again. He might even have been dead …Something, comforting although remote, was removed from his life never to return.

His silence tried Annie's nerves. She was so conscious of that brooding presence and far more conscious of the stillness in the cottage now than when she had lived in it alone.

She started when he entered the kitchen, even although she was expecting him, and when he did speak she stopped what she was doing so that she could listen more attentively.

Her amazement at seeing him puzzled and made him wonder. He had been brought up to accept himself as Malcolm Lamont, the offspring of one of Annie's cousins, now dead. But why should Annie look as though she had seen a fetch (wraith of a living person) when she saw her cousin's boy standing in the lobby?

One night when they were sitting together in the kitchen he asked her abruptly :

"Annie, wha am I?"

She looked up startled and one of her knitting-needles fell to the floor.

"Who are ye, Callum? Why now, Callum, ye're yoursel'."

"I ken that, but wha was ma faether?"

"I dinna ken," she faltered.

"Ye mean I was no born richt?"

"Ay, Callum, I mean that, but that was no your fault, Callum."

"Do ye ken wha ma mither was?"

"Ay," she answered reluctantly.

"Wha was she then?" he asked after a waiting pause.

"Ye'll promise noo that if I tell ye ye'll no tak ' advantage and try and find out mair?"

"Ay, I'll promise."

"Weel," said Annie, feeling very weak for telling him, "she is a minister's daughter."

"Oh, so she's living still," he answered deliberately. "And whit's her name, Annie?"

"Ye'll no be any the wiser kenning her name," she answered sharply. "Ye had better awa' to your bed noo."

So that was it, was it? His mother was a lady and had hidden him in Stonemerns with Annie Lamont and old Betsy Gaughan. He had been herding for those long years at Inchbuigh Farm, mucking byres, stamping on meal, when all the time he had been as good, no, better than his masters. She had left him at Stonemerns, permitted him to go as herd to a farm ...Probably she was married to another man now, had proper sons of her own. He hated those imagined boys even more than he hated his mother.

The following night, when he and Annie sat at the fire, he asked her as casually as he could :

"Annie, if ma mither was a lady, hoo did she come to leave me here?"

He asked questions so rarely that one always answered him more fully than one intended to do and regretted it afterwards. Also, so strong was his personality, Annie felt powerless to resist him.

"Weel,"she replied, "mither was servant to your mither's graund-mither." She had no sooner spoken than she wondered feverishly if she had said too much.

Callum's mind groped to remember names he had heard Betsy Gaughan mention.

"Your mither was servant to a family Brent in Edinburgh," he said thoughtfully.

"Noo, Callum," said Annie, troubled and vexed, "did ye no promise me last nicht no to gang prying and poking? Thinking of them things will no do ye any good or mak' ye any the happier, so think on ither things."

"If she's ma mither," he replied, sullen and resentful, "I should be happier—that I should. It's no richt I should be sent oot as——" He choked before continuing. "She should do something for me, it was she wha broucht me into the world, I didna ask to come."

"Na, na, Callum, that ye didna," said Annie, agitated at his distress.

"She should do something for me, should she no noo, Annie?"

"Mebbe," she muttered, "but o' course, Callum, she did keep ye here until ye were twelve and paid us richt handsome for ye too."

"And I'm near twenty noo," he cried, "that's eight year she's got aff. It's no richt at a' Ye maun do something aboot it for I am done wi' herding. I tell ye whit." His tone became confidential as a kettle's tune changes when it comes to the boil. "I'll write to her syne ye're no o'er fond o' writing."

"Ye'll do no such thing, Callum Lamont. Mind noo whit ye promised me last nicht."

"Weel, Annie," he pleaded, "ye'll write, will ye no? It's no richt."

"Na, na, Callum. A' she would do would be to send ye some money and I have enow for ye and for me."

"That willna do at a'," he replied mutinously. "Ye are to write to her and tell her aboot me and ask her whit is to happen to me. If ye dinna," he added with deliberate slowness, "I'll gang to Edinburgh and find oot whaur the Brents bide."

"Ye maun promise me that ye'll ne'er do that," said Annie, trembling. "It wouldna be richt, Callum, aifter she has kepit ye quiet a' them years. Ye've got it a' wrang aboot her, she'll no help ye anyway, ye're better standing by yoursel'."

"She'll have to help me, it's only richt that she should. Ye maun write to her and ask her whit she will do for me."

With trepidation and much heartburning, Annie penned a letter to Euphemia Gillespie, telling her that her son was once more at Stonemerns and had discovered whom he was, and asking her what was to become of him. She would not let Callum see the letter, but he asked so humbly to be allowed to take it to the mail himself that she consented.

Once out of sight of the cottage he memorized the name and address, noticing, his heart beating more quickly, that his mother was addressed on the envelope as "Miss," not "Mistress."

More silent than ever, he and Annie waited for an answer to come. The feeling of pity she had had for him as a baby swept over her again as she watched him now. He had always been so unchildishly strong, yet it was his very strength which made her heart contract as it would not have done had he been weaker, more tractable.

A reply came sooner than either had expected, for Euphemia, panic-stricken, wrote by return of mail. Annie stumblingly read it out word by word to Callum.

Annie must never again write so openly; if she had occasion to mention a certain person she must use the initials C. L. It was very painful for her to hear Annie's news and Annie was surely in a better position than she to know what was to be done. She could suggest nothing. Legally a certain person had no claims upon her but, as an act of grace, she was enclosing ten pounds. She would continue to send Annie ten pounds every year to be delivered to a certain person until such a time when he was able to do without any aid and on the strict understanding that a certain person should never, at any time in his life, try to get in touch with her personally or come to Barnfingal.

The emotions this letter raised in Callum were blacker because they were suppressed. He made no reply when Annie finished and, breathing as though she had run a distance, slowly fitted the letter into its envelope. He despised this woman who could write so coldly, he hated her with a hate so strong he wanted to do her some violent hurt. To think of those twenty years which lay behind him, empty, frustrated, wasted; to think that all she was prepared to do for him in the future was to pay him ten pounds to keep him away from her ...

A feeling of crushing depression oppressed his spirit in the days that followed. The lonely moors, the squalid cottages, the poverty all around him, the monotonous voices of Annie and the villagers which held the desolation of years, all weighed him with a terrible sense of meaninglessness dragging itself out to an inevitable end.

He told Annie he had best go and find work to do, he thought he would go to a city this time. She agreed, and it was arranged he should leave on Wednesday's coach for Halkeith, the nearest big town. He did not think it necessary to tell her that he was going to descend from the coach at Turner's Dyke and take another one to Dormay, which he ascertained was the nearest point to Barnfingal to which the coaches drove.

He told himself as he jolted about on the coach seat that he had best change his name. He went over in his mind all the ones he could think of at the moment: MacAlpine, Bain, MacOuat, Crearar, Macintosh, Taggart, Stewart. He paused when he thought of Stewart, that clan of kings and tinkers, then sweated when he realized that for a second he had considered taking that name which belonged to Fiona and to three doomed, scattered families. He must forget about Fiona, he must answer her letters as shortly as he could, until in time they drifted irrevocably apart. He must not allow his heart to cry out to her over the cruel, lonely miles that separated them. Her name was the last he must take. But he did not want to use any of these others which belonged to men who were now homeless and friendless. He wanted a name he had never heard of before, which had no associations for him.

There was only one other passenger, who occupied the top of the coach with him. This was a haggard man with sucked-in cheeks who was cleaning out his pipe with the point of his knife. Something in the man's interested, contented attitude made Callum resentful; he could not share his peace of mind so he felt the urgent desire to destroy it. He leant forward and asked him what his name was, fixing him intently with his eyes as though daring him to look startled. But the man was an amiable soul and, his face cracking into a grin, answered readily enough:

"Willie Goullie."

Callum was conscious of a sense of shock. Goullie! No, no, that would never do. Besides, he thought, anxious of any excuse to avoid taking it, it was an unusual name. People would stare at anyone called that, question one about it, ask where one came from, and if there were anything he hated more than being questioned it was being stared at. But the very next name he saw or heard he would take, no matter what it was.

The man opposite was smiling vacantly out of nervousness. Callum, who suspected he was laughing at him, gave him a look that made the sheepish grin quiver from his face.

He saw it written in white paint on an old barrel at the roadside—Armit. Yes, that would do. He had no memories about anyone called Armit and no associations with a broken barrel turned upside-down at the wayside.

Chapter Eight

HIS destination lay farther inland than Gilhead and he had to travel by several coaches. He arrived at Dormay late one afternoon and took the road which led by the side of a Loch to Barnfingal. The Loch was a complete surprise to him and he could scarcely take his eyes from it. At one place, where the road wound so near the water it must constantly have been flooded, he stopped for a long time only to watch the little white waves which lifted, fell forward and broke on the shingly shore. Sometimes, if he held his head a certain way, he caught sight of a transient rainbow caught in the waves' spray. It was so fleeting that each time he saw it he wondered if it really had been and paused to catch sight of it once again.

This country was more desolate than Gilhead, more cut off from the rest of the world. He saw no cottages until he came to Barnfingal, and there they did not cluster in friendly little groups but were scattered far up the glen. There was no church that he could see except the ruined gable of one standing on a hill beside a rounded graveyard. For one sickening moment he wondered if he had been too late, if the church had crumbled, the manse been shut up, and his mother flown. Then he realized that the ruin was a very old one and remembered that his mother had written only a few weeks ago from the manse.

He went into one of the cottages and the woman gave him something to eat. In answer to his remark that they must be reel bad in them parts syne they had no kirk, she told him that indeed they had a kirk which lay two miles along the road, exactly halfway between Barnfingal and Auchendee. Ay, and the manse was alongside o'it. When he heard her speak so confidently of the manse, his heart leapt wildly within him and he was seized by a feeling of uncontrollable excitement. He felt he could eat nothing more, but he put the scones she had spread for him into his pockets.

He began to walk in great haste along the road as though he did not expect the manse to wait for him, but even in his haste he felt this place was answering him. He would have liked to have owned a farm here, to have forced the grudging earth to yield to him its richest until he had towering crops and giant haystacks. He would have built it exactly where that farm was standing on a hill, for he liked to think he was on the top of things; besides it was facing the wild, grey Loch so that he could see it at different times of the day from different windows.

Despite his hurry to reach the manse, he branched off from the high road and took the overgrown path which led to the farm. As he approached he felt there was something strange about it, when he reached it he saw it was deserted. No one lived in it now. Its house was untenanted by people, its sheds and byres by animals, its lofts and barns by grain and hay.

He could tell from the size everything was that it had once been prosperous and he found himself resenting it was in such disrepair. As far as he could judge it had lain unoccupied for years, but surely it would not take very much to make it habitable again. Its state of dilapidation annoyed him so much that he longed to begin to set it to rights himself.

A door, hanging on one hinge, swung in the wind. He went forward and closed it, placing a great boulder against it to keep it shut. He saw that it would not be long before the remaining hinge gave way and the rotting door fell. Then the wind would break into the house, sound on the wooden stairs, call up the unlit chimneys, swirl dust from the corners, make holes in spiders' webs ...

Nothing on earth would have induced him to enter that house, but he did climb into a loft, bending his head unthinkingly to avoid the top of the low lintel. He determined he would come and sleep there that night. He sat down in one corner, for he felt suddenly, overwhelmingly tired although he had only walked the few miles from Dormay. Whenever he did not feel himself, he was thrown into a state of unreasonable depression. There was a beam of wood across the floor which, if he had been a man of six feet, he could have rested his feet against, but he was short and his feet fell nowhere near it. He felt a draught above his head and, looking up, saw a narrow slit through which the wind whistled. Lit up by the weak shaft of light was something ingrained in the wall. He knelt to see what it could be and found it was deeply-carved initials. They were placed inside a swollen, uneven heart, and he traced their legend to run "D.Gow," and below that "E.G."

He descended from the loft and walked down the path to the road. The square toe of his boot kicked against something and he stooped to pick it up. It was only an earthy potato, but he turned it over in his hand before putting it down. It had suddenly struck him as odd that a potato lived under the ground all its life, its many eyes beholding only darkness.

He felt very hot, so he knelt beside a moss burn at the wayside and plunged his hands into it to cool himself. Drops of moisture dripped perpetually from the narrow bank into the water. He knew the trout taken from these moss burns were always black like the water they lived in. Fearful for a moment, he compared himself, being illegitimate, to those trout born in moss burns. But that could not be, that could not be, it was not his fault he was not born right, except for that he was just like other people. He raised himself and began to walk once more hurriedly towards the manse.

He could not see it from the road, but when he came to a gate at one side he opened it, for he knew it was about two miles from Barnfingal. He walked down a steep, wayward path which was strewn with cones and pine needles. Ay, he had been quite right. The manse was down here at the Loch's edge, closely surrounded by trees, almost as though it were hiding. He crept nearer and nearer. It was quite unpretentious and much smaller than he had expected—why, Inchbuigh farmhouse was bigger by far. He was aware of a feeling of vague disappointment. He was so near it now that he could touch its grey walls. He gripped the sill of a window tightly with his fingers and cautiously drew himself up.

For a long time he stared into the room at three figures grouped round the fire, so engrossed that he did not hear the sound of wheels rapidly approaching along the not far distant road. At last he turned away, angry and sick at heart. Although he did not know it, he was nearer tears than he had ever been.

Book Three

Chapter One

"*SO* like Glen, isn't she? *No* Lucy that I can see."

The little niece had been taken upstairs to rest after her long, tiring journey and the three aunts were gathered in the living-room round the fire, for, although it was early summer, the atmosphere was damp.

"It's her colouring that makes her so pretty," Euphemia continued in her staccato, italicized speech. Then she exclaimed, starting up excitedly, "Oh, how stupid of us. We forgot to show her the way to pull out that broken top drawer. I had better go up at —"

"For heaven's sake, Euphie, don't disturb her," Alice said impatiently. "The child is half dead with fatigue and isn't thinking of unpacking just now. I drew her curtains and she's lying down."

"I wonder," Euphemia said reflectively after a pause, "if she will like being here."

"No, I'm quite sure she won't," Alice replied with decision.

"Lucy didn't," reminded Elizabeth.

"But Glen always seemed so glad to come home," said Euphemia.

"Darling Glen," whispered Elizabeth, a tremor passing over her face.

"He was always so full of enthusiasm" said Euphemia, looking mistily in front of her.

"He took that from mamma," commented Alice.

"He had the gladdest laugh on earth," said Elizabeth.

"It's so hard to think he is lying under there, cold and still and silent," said Euphemia, shuddering.

But Elizabeth could not imagine Glen lying still and silent, confined in a black coffin. Instead she thought of him being borne past outside on the hollow wind, shouting splendidly at nothing.

She was delicate and spent all her days now on a couch. Sometimes she felt she was going much quicker than the motion of the earth, but these were not so bad as the days when she felt the earth was going much quicker than she. At other times she escaped from her tired body and felt in perfect rhythm with it.

Someone had once told her that she was very patient. She had looked up mockingly and said, "Some are born patient, some attain patience, but oh, the Lord help those who have patience thrust upon them."

When people spoke of her sister Alice they unconsciously hushed their voices, for it was well known she no longer lived with her husband. The fact that he was a minister with one of the largest parishes in Glasgow, made the situation even worse. It was she who was blamed, for no one could understand how any woman could fail to agree with one so courtly, so amiable, so altogether praiseworthy as Francis MacMillan. Alice, however, had long ceased to care what people thought about her. She pleased herself entirely, and so her life was restless and dissatisfied, for of all people she found herself the most difficult to please.

She walked as though she leant against the wind, and was tall, with a smooth, good-looking face. Every man was a challenge to her; she had that dangerous charm which made them feel in her presence like chevaliers. Her youngest sister Euphemia looked years her senior. A nervous, thin, overwrought woman, she often found herself thanking people when properly they should have been thanking her. She was trying to live with and was under the maddening impression that no one had ever endured so much as she. She would listen to other people's troubles, she might even condole with them, but always her sympathy was qualified. She had no head for heights and a total lack of concentration; her face was lined, her voice high-pitched. Her harassing temperament never permitted her to enjoy anything while it was happening although no one could anticipate or look back with keener pleasure than she. It was her way of baulking life.

"Her godmother will be sure to invite her to Edinburgh," Alice said thoughtfully, reverting to the subject of their niece.

"That *will* be nice for her," affirmed Euphemia.

"When did Mr. Rand say he would come to see papa?" inquired Alice.

"He gave no definite date, all he said was he thought it would be some time within the next few weeks."

The door opened and Mr. Gillespie entered, a wiry man with huddled shoulders and the fretful, unhealthy look of the chronic dyspeptic. He still cried Wolf, read his books and peppered them with neat marginal notes and question marks. He preached long, cantankerous sermons every Sabbath, droned out the service for the dead, and with equal gloom, but more rarely, droningly united in marriage.

He was a man who lived by rote, but to-day his habits had been interrupted, for he had gone to meet his granddaughter at Davar to bring her to the manse. Now that he had returned he could not settle in his room and instead wandered uneasily about the house. "A lost day, a lost day," he repeatedly told himself.

With the passing years he found it increasingly difficult to adapt himself to the few changes in his uneventful life. He still spoke to his daughters as though they were young misses of eighteen and nineteen instead of middle-aged women. It had been only to-day, when he saw his unknown grandchild was dressed in mourning, that he realized Glen was dead. The realization disturbed and troubled him. He felt like a rebuke on earth, felt that somewhere he was being criticized. He had lived long past his allotted span, yet his son had died in the midst of his triumphant life. He felt Glen had stolen a march on him—Glen, whom he used to accuse of never finishing anything he began.

He wanted to be comforted, he wanted someone to tell him that it was absolutely imperative he should go on living, but he could not turn to any of his daughters. They were always so bracing with him and he hated nothing more than to be braced. It would have been different had his wife been alive and he could have drawn on her inexhaustible wells of sympathy, but years ago she had left the manse for the smallest house of all.

He fidgeted about the room, infecting them with his restlessness until they were glad when at last he left, muttering he had some work to do. He went into his shabby study and straightened all the chairs. A wave of industry swept over him and he began to tidy out the cupboard, which smelt overpoweringly of fust and damp and mould. He had no sooner strewn the contents round him on the floor, however, than he regretted his rash assiduity. It would take him hours to arrange them and put them back. Euphemia really must do it, she had far more time at her disposal than he.

He straightened himself, and as he did so his foot kicked against a wooden box, which rattled. Irritably he stooped to pick it up. Scrawled across the top in a childish, unformed hand were the words "Elizabeth and Glen Gillespie." He slid off the lid and looked inside in his inquisitive way. Lying within were a few odd dominoes. Something quite incomprehensible jerked at his heart as he turned them over with his fingers.

What had happened to those little eager hands, with the old-fashioned smocked cuffs, which had played with the now yellowed dominoes? Death had laid its palsied touch on the strongest long, long before they grew old and wrinkled, yet missed the slimmest and most delicate of all. Life had so bewildered a third, which had always rather grabbed at the double sixes, that now they slightly shook, and a fourth had grown plump and quite forgotten how dominoes were played.

Chapter Two

A GATE barred the manse path from the road, and sitting on the gate, idly swinging her foot, was a young girl dressed entirely in black with heavy bands of crape round the skirt of her frock. The afternoon was very quiet but its unearthly silence was at last disturbed by the rumbling of cart wheels. The noise was so remote that at first she wondered if it were only a delusion, but as it came nearer and nearer the surrounding silence intensified it until it sounded like the rumbling of several carts instead of one.

The girl did not rouse herself from her preoccupation but continued to hum below her breath and drowsily watch the lumbering cart approach. A man was thudding along beside the horse. Her half-closed grey eyes looked down into his black ones gazing darkly up at her from under an overhanging brow. As the cart passed, however, her eyes widened with surprise and she sat upright on the gate, looking wonderingly over her shoulder, for the expression of the man gazing up at her had been almost baleful.

She stared after the cart and horse until they disappeared. Who could he be, that strange, dark man, and why should he look at her so uglily? Then she told herself he was some labourer, of course, and dismissed him from her mind, for to Lilith Gillespie when one was a labourer one began and ended there.

She slid from the gate and yawned, for she had grown weary with keeping still so long. She had been sitting there since three o'clock, when she had waved good-bye to Aunt Alice, who was going abroad for a time. Alice was unsettled and rarely remained in the same place for long; her restless mind demanded constant movement and change in her surroundings. Her old home depressed her. It was like a tomb to Alice, a tomb of young hopes and frail, breath-catching memories, a tomb which imprisoned the only thing in her life that had remained dear to her. Had it not been for her sister Elizabeth, she would never have returned to Barnfingal even on erratic visits.

Lilith did think Aunt Alice might have taken her with her instead of going with Louisa Brownlie. She could have paid for herself, she thought proudly, for although her father had left her not a penny, she inherited a little money from her mother. Lilith was hazy as to the money's whereabouts but she derived a great deal of moral comfort from the knowledge that it was hers. Yes, she did think Aunt Alice might have taken her. Of course it was only three months since her father had died, and perhaps it would not be very seemly to go sight-seeing so soon, but she was sure her father, if he had known, would have been the very one to be pleased. She sighed deeply and ran her finger along the rough top bar of the gate.

It was only three months since her brilliant, tentative father had died, leaving behind him a generous will, no money and an accumulation of debts. It was only six weeks ago since she had come to the manse. Only six weeks! It seemed like a lifetime. London, her father, their home, belonged to another existence. It was all so different, this new life in the old manse with its damp walls and tree-shaded rooms, the watching stillness of the countryside, the grey Loch mirroring the surrounding mountains as though to impress them twice on her unwilling brain, the wet Highland weather....

She started down the path to the manse, when she paused. The sound of wheels, lighter and swifter than those of a cart, and the rapid trotting of horses' hoofs on a hard road broke the silence. She turned quickly and mounted the gate again, eagerly gazing in the direction from which the sounds were coming. It was an excitement nowadays even to watch a vehicle passing on the road.

The carriage drew nearer and nearer, coming towards her as though its occupants had stirring news to impart. She sighed once more, this time unconsciously, then her heart missed a beat, for the plunging horses were drawn up just outside the gate. Perhaps she was only going to be asked how much farther it was to Auchendee or Moreneck ...But no, the door was opened and a man descended. He dismissed the carriage, telling the driver to be back for him at seven, turned quickly, saw her and stopped.

He looked at her keenly for a moment, then he smiled and, bowing, introduced himself as Napier Rand. He had come, he said, to see Mr. Gillespie about a most important charge for whom he was trustee and, if he did not mistake, that very charge was standing before him. She answered that indeed she was Lilith Gillespie and began to say it was very good of him to make so inconvenient a journey on her behalf, but she grew tongue-tied in the middle. He opened the gate and they walked down the path together. She answered him only in monosyllables, for he was the assured, businesslike kind of person who made one feel full of muddled thoughts and half-finished sentences.

She took him into the living-room, where he was introduced to Aunt Elizabeth and Aunt Euphemia. Unconsciously he lowered his voice, for the Miss Gillespie on the couch looked to him as though loud voices and sudden noises would shatter her frail being into fragments.

He was a susceptible young man although appearances belied him. He had a clever, handsome face if a somewhat proud bearing, but his arrogance was only a protection for his sensitiveness. He had grown, perhaps, a little too fastidious. Things had been spoiled for him by coming too easily, he had never had to strive for anything he wanted, no demands had ever been made of him. He was like an engineer who has never had necessity to put his excellent machinery into action.

Mr. Gillespie was told of his arrival and saw him in his study, where they discussed the best security in which to place Lilith's small capital. The minister's fussing indecision fretted the younger man, who never had the slightest difficulty about making up his mind. He was a lawyer by profession and liked everything cut and dried. He had scarcely known Glen Gillespie, but Glen, dashing off his will, had written down the name Napier Rand as he somehow felt it was necessary for at least one of his trustees to be in stable circumstances. Glen had never had any head for business but he had an instinct about the best way to rid himself of responsibility. Lilith used to hear him talk about a stingy old beggar called Uncle Benjamin who would be sure to leave her his money, but Uncle Benjamin, it seemed, died and bequeathed all his fortune to Foreign Missions. Lilith would have been entirely dependent on her relations if Lucy, her mother, had not been careful to leave her, in a prim little will, all she possessed, which, by prudent investment, had now grown into a comparatively large sum.

After Rand had very decisively reassured Mr. Gillespie that he did consider what he was proposing was for the best, he returned to the living-room, where he prepared to make himself amenable to the three Miss Gillespies. He had never met his mother's godchild before and he thought her an appealing little thing. It was her colouring which made her so pretty, the soft brightness of her brown hair, the delicate tinting of her complexion, and the clarity of her eyes. He was to discover that at times she could look even enchanting.

Aunt Euphemia poured out tea and leaned towards him over the table in her anxiety to know if it were the strength he liked it. He admitted she was nice but he found her very exhausting; her intenseness seemed to drain all the vitality from him. Her slightest words were weighted with earnestness and she spoke with such energy one felt she was protecting herself against possible dispute. Despite all her intensity, she was distraite, as though she were always dwelling on something that happened long ago. She was so busy thinking of what next to say that she never listened to what was said to her.

She felt fluttered and excited that afternoon, for here was, she thought, the very man—good looks, good family, good position—to marry little Lilith. Lilith, with the agonizing sensitiveness of youth, divined her thoughts and prayed that he would not. She grew shy and awkward again as she waited on tenterhooks for what her aunt would say next, and she pouted with vexation when she heard her declare that Lilith really *must* put on her hat and take Mr. Rand to see the Loch.

She had nothing to say to him as she led him to the little stony beach and she felt cross and angry with her well-meaning relative for placing her in such a position. He sat on a boulder and she on the stump of a tree, the skirts of her full black dress falling round her, while the water lapped at the loose pebbles on the shore. Above them the leafy branches of the trees moved gently in the wind as though playing an invisible instrument. Lilith often came here when she was alone. Woefully she would gaze across the Loch as though she imagined it and the mountains were there solely for the purpose of banishing her from the rest of the world, but at the water's edge she did not feel so lonely as when she wandered across wild moors and climbed bleak hills. Often, sitting on some windy height, she had felt she wanted to lift up her face and weep at the loneliness of it all. The mountains with their shadowed concaves, the sad, beaten-looking hills all around her, made her full of fear.

Her companion stirred beside her and his voice broke in upon her thoughts.

"My mother would be so delighted," he said, "if you would come to visit her in the near future."

She forgot everything else as she turned to smile her gratitude at him, her little face lit up with a wistful eagerness.

He told himself that evening as he drove away that he must see to it his mother invited her soon—'pon his soul, he must.

"Such a charming man," said Aunt Euphemia after the carriage had disappeared.

But Lilith did not answer, somehow she did not feel inclined to discuss him with her. She ran across the road to pick some bluebells for her Aunt Elizabeth and was on her way back when Euphemia heard her exclaim sharply,

"Oh, there he is again."

"Who, dear?"

Her aunt's eyes followed her gaze to the square figure of a man coming towards them down the road.

"What about him, dear?"

"Nothing—only—I—think there is something odd about him. He looks at one so queerly."

"He cannot be a native, for I have never seen him here before," her aunt remarked.

The man passed between them in silence, pretending not to see them.

Lilith was absent-minded that evening, for she kept thinking of all the things she might have said to Mr. Rand. Outside it was very still. The little wind which had played at the Loch's edge in the afternoon had calmed into complete motionless. Not a breath of air stirred the fraught-looking trees which stood so near the windows. When a green leaf fell, as though grown too heavy, it made a sound and the snapping of a twig was three times intensified in the stillness.

Lilith became restless and wanted to go for a little walk, but Aunt Euphemia said the night air was bad for her. A haze rose from the Loch and the darkness crept closer and closer to the manse, blurring the distances, enfolding the trees in blue mists, deepening and darkening as it drew nearer.

At nine o'clock Bella brought in Lilith's glass of hot milk, muttering and grunting away to herself like an old witch, as she always did, even when not particularly displeased. Bella had frightened Lilith at first, but now she felt quite at home with her even although she could scarcely make out a word she said in her incomprehensible jargon of dadleys, snecks, dytes. ...

At the dreaded hour of ten Grandpapa rose and locked up the house. He tapped at the weather-glass in the narrow hall and told them, gloomily triumphant, through the open door that it was falling, then he came into the room to put out the lamp.

Lilith's bedroom seemed full of unexpected creaks and little cracking sounds that night. She wished her Aunt Alice were sharing it with her. A large furry moth, which terrified her as much as a runaway horse would have done, was trapped in the room. It moved its clumsy wings weakly in the candle flame, which flared up and turned blue. Something sizzled and then fell with a little thud to the floor. Lilith sickened and stood on a chair to blow out the light in case she touched the moth with her bare feet.

Chapter Three

IT was afternoon and Callum was having a belated dinner in the cottage of Janet and Enoch MacDiarmid at Auchendee, where he now lived. He had found it difficult to procure work in the district, for there were native men in plenty, but he had at last secured employment from the Marquis of Moreneck's grieve. It was chiefly carter's work, to be true, but he had to be if not grateful at least acquiescent with his lot.

Auchendee was a tiny clachan of white-washed cottages gathered together at the foot of an enormous, rounded, unfriendly, green hill. A tumultous burn sounded down the glen. The MacDiarmid's cottage faced the burn and its three-cornered garden ran steeply to the very edge of the precipitous bank. Stiff blue delphiniums towered above the crumbling dyke that surrounded it and in summer it was filled with the ceaseless drone of bees, for Janet kept four straw skeps. In one corner was a well so overgrown with verdure that the sun could not penetrate to it and its water even on the hottest day was always icily cold.

Towards the end of summer, when anyone entered the cottage, he scattered petals and withered heads as he brushed them with his sleeve. Its walls could not be seen in the front because of the flowers which clustered round the windows, hung over the doorway, and clung to the rough stones and thatch. The tropæolum even trailed its crimson flowers and pointed leaves through a crack in the wall into the kitchen, where Janet trained it to frame the window.

The cottage had its back to the brae and was sunk below its level, so that looking out of the tiny kitchen window one saw the grasses waving far above the distant mountains, and only the feet and ankles of those journeying up and down the rutted road. So expert was Janet now that she could tell Enoch, who was slower on the uptake, whether the passing scratched, brown legs were Maggie Crerar's or her sister Jean's, and whether the heavy, mud-encrusted boots belonged to the shepherd or to the ploughman.

A shadow crossed over the window and Callum and Janet looked up involuntarily in time to see the uneven hem of a black skirt and a pair of woman's boots, down-trodden at the heel, pass the window.

"Teenie MacIntyre, if I'm no mista'en," muttered Janet.

Callum knew Teenie by sight and had learnt to know her by reputation, for she was notorious as a clasher (gossip). She was a loosely-jointed woman with a head that nodded and arms that napped at her sides like some broken, mechanical doll's. She was like the drawing, come alive, absently sketched on blotting-paper. Whenever the crofters saw that Teenie had donned her black skirt they knew she was about to stravaig (go about aimlessly and idly) at one of their cottages and watched with trepidation which she would choose. Janet MacDiarmid had neither time nor patience for her, but custom demanded that the unwelcome guest should be greeted as though welcome.

"Come awa' ben, Teenie," she said, "and have a seat to yoursel'. Ye'll be warm trapesing up yon brae. Will ye have a dish o' tea?"

"Oh, dinna heed."

"Ye micht as weel—it's in the pot,"

"Oh weel, I'm no for minding."

Janet poured out tea for her visitor and filled up the silent Callum's cup at the table. He was eating very slowly, for he wanted to spin out his meal as long as possible. Never before, since he had come to Auchendee, had he had an opportunity to listen to a gossip and he did so want that gossip to be about what he wished to hear. He glowered fixedly at the back of Teenie's oblong head while he stirred his tea as though it were a plum pudding, and concentrated laboriously on the manse and its occupants, in an attempt to communicate the remembrance of them to her. And sure enough, after a few desultory remarks about thunder in the air, silly Teenie MacIntyre felt an almost overwhelming desire to discuss their minister and his family.

"So the meenister has his graund-docther biding wi' him noo," she remarked.

"Ay, so he has."

"She's a shilpit (pale) bit thing."

"Aweel, a toon bairn has no the chances o' a country bairn."

"She's no so bonny as Miss Alice was," went on Teenie.

"She was always so blythe, Miss Alice," Janet said reflectively.

"She disna come back often noo," commented Teenie, "and ye ne'er see Miss Elizabeth at a'."

"I mind when we used to see them a' in the kirk," said Janet, smiling reminiscently into the fire," and I used to think I had ne'er seen a row o' bonnier faces."

"The boy's deith maun have been a sad blow to the meenister—his only son too. The peety is it's no a son he leaves ahind him, only a girl."

"Aweel, mayhap they would no change her for a' the sons in the world."

"Na, neether they would," Teenie agreed emphatically, the firelight shining on her polished face." They do say as she's got money ahind her and that she will be quite weel-to-do aince she's twenty-one. She'll need it, for she'll no get muckle frae the meenister when he dees. They're in a puir way, but I've heard it said that if they had wasted less they would have mair noo. They were broucht up like ladies o' quality and no like a puir meenister's dochters. I mind when Mistress Gillespie was alive she had to gang to Edinburgh on law business and left Miss Alice wi' the hoose on her hands. She had to pay Bella her wages, and Bella got eleven pound the year but Miss Alice couldna divide eleven by twelve, so she juist raised Bella's wages to twelve pound the year."

"Weel, weel, and that was a graund way oot o' it."

"Ay, to thems that has the money. And if Miss Alice did no gang and order a leg o' beef frae MacAnally's in mistake for a leg o' mutton. If she had kent mair aboot a hoose she micht have kepit her husband for langer. They do say as they have French blood in them, and they maun have something extraordinar', for ye mind there was something queer aboot Miss Euphemia."

"I canna say I mind onything o' the sort," replied Janet MacDiarmid. "Is your tea oot, Teenie? And wha was at the van last nicht? Is that ye awa' then, Malcolm? I'll leave your mug o' milk and a scone on the dresser for ye, and mind to turn the key in the lock when ye come ben to-nicht for there are gipsies doon at the Loch."

Callum shut the door behind him and walked down the brae. The air was heavy with approaching thunder and an unnatural calm pervaded the atmosphere. He struck from the brae on to the road, for his work took him to most of the clachans on the north side of the Loch. He walked at a steady pace, his gaze never wandering from the ground at his feet, while he thought his brooding thoughts. When he came to the humpbacked bridge which led over what was known as the manse burn, he paused, assailed by sudden thirst. He descended the bank and was about to lie down and plunge his mouth into the water when he stopped short.

A little farther up the bank, on the opposite side, sat a girl dressed all in black except for a yellow straw hat, but even it had a black scarf swathed round it. She had been paddling, for her shoes and stockings lay beside her on the bank and she now sat with her bare pink legs stretched out in front of her, dipping only her heels in the tumbling water.

Something made her glance up with swift apprehension and she caught him looking across at her. She flushed under the shadow of her broad-brimmed hat and gazed at him with the resentment of one who discovers she has been watched when she thought herself alone. She would have given much at that moment to have been in a dignified attitude, with her bare feet safely covered by shoes and stockings. He continued to stare at her so intently, however, for his thoughts moved with painful slowness, that she was secretly flattered. Her self-possession returned and she felt like some great lady amazing a yokel who had never seen her like before.

"Do you wish anything?" she asked proudly.

"Ay," he answered, "I cam' for a drink," and he knelt down on the opposite bank. But he did not dip his face into the burn, instead he scooped up the water to his mouth with one broad hand.

His answer disconcerted her somewhat, but while he was bending his head she drew up her feet and hid them under her skirts. She watched him gravely, as a child might watch a donkey drink, and when he had finished she remarked politely,

"It is thirsty weather, is it not?"

"It's no the weather has made me thirsty," he replied definitely. "I had braxy to ma dinner."

She had no reply to make to this, but he did not move away and somehow she did not expect him to.

"Do you live here?" she ventured at last.

"Ay, I bide at Auchendee."

"But you are not a native of this place, are you?" she pursued. "My aunt said she had never seen you here before." She could have bitten out her tongue after she had spoken. It seemed as though she had been so interested in him and of course she had only spoken and thought of him quite inadvertently.

"Na," he answered slowly, choosing his words with care as though afraid he were going to be surprised into giving something away, "I'm no a native o' this place—I juist cam' a wee while back."

"And do you like being here?" she asked, thinking she was taking a kindly interest in him, for he struck her as being very much alone.

"I dinna ken that I like it," he returned, still in the same slow, momentous voice, "but I have to bide here for the noo."

"Why?"

He felt like a horse which has been pulled up too sharply, every nerve jarred. His jaw set and he did not reply to her question. She was sorry for him, imagining his silence implied that beggars could not be choosers.

A single large drop of rain fell and splashed on to her lap. She lifted her face and looked up questioningly at the sky.

"Why," she said, dismayed, "it's raining."

"Ay," he answered, almost contemptuously, "there was a fu' rainbow in the north this morning and it's been drawing to rain a' day. There will be a graund thunder-plump soon."

The words were scarcely out of his mouth when a distant clap of thunder reverberated amongst the hollow-sounding mountains. The rain began to fall heavily in large, cold drops.

"Ye'll get wet," he remarked, watching her.

"I'm afraid so," she replied quite apologetically, feeling somehow inadequate for the situation.

"Ye had better gang under the bridge," he said, "and put on your shoes and stockings there."

"Yes," she agreed readily, grateful for any suggestion, "I can wait there until it's dry."

"Ye'll be biding there a' nicht then, for the rain's on for guid. But if ye gang under the bridge I'll gang doon to the manse and fetch a coat to put o'er ye."

This suggestion, coming from him, surprised her; somehow she had thought he would not have liked to approach the manse. She rose and began to walk unsteadily beside the burn's edge, but she made little progress. The pebbles hurt her bare feet, the boulders were slippery and she was nervous, for she knew he was watching her. She felt, quite incomprehensibly, that she wanted to cry.

He crossed the burn and lifted her in his arms, carrying her with ease to under the bridge. She hated herself for not hating to be touched by him. Her heart beat so wildly that she felt it would choke her and she prayed he would not notice it.

Under the arch it was clammy and cold and gloomy. She felt sure it was just the place where there would be rats, and she did not want to be left alone, but she dared not confide this to her companion. So she waited for him under the low bridge. Moisture oozed from between the slimy stones, trickling down their sides, and she noticed that some little ferns had taken root between them. She was not imaginative, but she found herself marvelling at these little ferns growing in the dark in all their fairy-like perfection for no one to see. Already the torrential rain had swollen the burn, which brawled past her with increased eagerness. Soon there would be no dry stone on which to stand. She kept giving little involuntary shudders, for she found it very damp.

She heard his returning footsteps and a minute later saw him coming towards her. They had given him her thick black cape and the antiquated manse umbrella to keep it dry. He handed her the cape and she wanted to pout at his remissness for not helping her into it. It was difficult to clamber up the slippery bank and quite impossible for her to hold the heavy umbrella over her head, so that by the time she reached the road the rain had weighted down the brim of her hat all round her flushed face. She put out her hand from her cape and pushed it back from her forehead. He glared at her wrist which, he told himself, was as thin as a hen's leg. He was quite sure he could snap it with one hand.

He made no move to open the gate for her, and she hoped she did not betray her surprise that he was not going to accompany her at least a little of the way, but she thought him very rude nevertheless. She felt she would have to say something, however, so she merely thanked him formally over the gate and said coldly she hoped she had not kept him late.

"No," he answered, "I pass here every nicht about the same time."

She wished passionately as she turned to walk down the path that he had not told her that. She hoped she did not look very ridiculous and she hid her sopping hat as much as possible with the umbrella. She wished they had given him her cape with the silk braid instead of this old heavy affair. Then she told herself indignantly that it was he, not she, who should be feeling ridiculous.

Chapter Four

A ROISTERING autumn wind sounded through the glen. It stripped the black trees of their remaining shrivelled leaves which threw little flying shadows on the ground as, circling, they fluttered down to be soaked in rain puddles or blown in impetuous, rustling brown herds. It drove furrows in the sheeps' wool, revealing it to be a pure yellow under the matted grey, and made stormy the moody Loch. Above, the sky was high and blue, with white clouds chasing across it.

Callum was walking beside his horse and cart, piled with turnips he was taking to Auchendee. He was gazing at the ground, and the sun, shining brilliantly on the wet road, pitted it with ruby shadows before his dazzled eyes.

Suddenly he jerked his head upwards as a hideous screeching sound rent the air. He had heard that noise once before, for one morning he had passed the gipsies' encampment and seen them lying sleeping on the ground, tightly wrapped up like mummies. Only a brood of tattered children and one dishevelled woman were stirring. She was deaf and dumb, and when her children could not understand what she wanted she made angry, screeching sounds.

Callum had heard the gipsies were leaving that day, to the crofters' relief, and when he turned the bend in the road he saw them gathered in a group ready to start with their one rickety, heaped cart. As he drew nearer he noticed all their attention was riveted on the one spot, so intently they did not hear his approach. Then to his amazement he saw that against the tree they were staring at stood Lilith Gillespie, her face white and her body shrinking. They were trying to reassure her, to tell her they had not meant to frighten her, they had only wanted to see her bonny face, to know if she would like to cross their hand with silver, mebbe; and the more they tried to reassure her the nearer they pressed round the tree and the quicker they jabbered. The smell of them sickened her, her eyes glanced frantically from one to another, trying to seek one who would understand that all she wanted was to get away, but her gaze only met a sea of covert, copper faces lit by dark, mysterious eyes.

Then her glance fell on Callum standing in the middle of the road and she felt towards him as one feels when, stranded in a foreign land, one lights unexpectedly upon a fellow-countryman. She withdrew from the cringing, ingratiating gipsies and backed towards him until she stood at his side and he could feel her sleeve lightly touching his.

Someone said something to the bony pony harnessed to the cart and it jerked forward with its miscellaneous load. The gipsies formed into an uneven procession behind and followed it. Lilith watched them as, smiling, they filed past her. How could they live, those dirty people with their wild, staring children whose rags blew in the wind? Surely, surely they could not feel the cold and damp as she would feel it. And Callum wondered as they passed him what ancient secret it was they hid fast locked in their dusky breasts as they wandered outcasts over the earth, what bond it was that kept them always together as one tribe, what their watching eyes really saw....

When the last one had disappeared over the crest of the hill, Lilith began to explain at length why she had been so frightened.

"They came round about me so," she said, "and I thought they were going to steal from me, and then I thought they would be angry when they saw I had nothing on me to take. But I had, you know," she told him childishly, opening her shut hand to disclose a slender silver chain." Papa gave me that, and when I saw them coming I took it off and hid it behind my back."

He put up his hand for the horse's rope rein and made a guttural sound to it in his throat.

"Where are you going?" she demanded, annoyed he was paying so little attention to her.

"To Auchendee."

"Is that your horse?" she inquired in order to detain him.

"Ay."

"You mean it is your master's horse," she corrected.

He looked at her, moving his head slowly, as he always did, as though he had a crick in his neck.

"Syne ye ken it is ma maister's horse, why ask me if it is mine?" he answered.

"Just to hear what you would say," she said, a little gaspily.

A silence fell between them until she broke it by remarking confidentially,

"I was going down to the Loch—I'm making a little bower there, you know, but I can't get the branches of the trees to bend as I want them to. Will you come and do it for me?"

He did not reply, but he moved the horse to the side of the road where it could graze, then he followed his companion to the edge of the Loch. She led him to a large, flat boulder which was to serve for a seat and which she had covered with moss ("It looks just like green velvet, doesn't it?" she asked him proudly), and she wanted him to bend the branches of the trees above it to form an arch over her head.

She stood to one side and watched him critically as he did it, while leaves rained down all round him.

"That is as guid as ye'll get it," he said at last.

"Oh, is it as good as you can do?"she asked disappointedly, with emphasis. "Well, I suppose it is. What a pity you are not taller and could reach to that nice thin branch up there."

"I didna mak' masel'," he replied.

"No, of course you didn't," she agreed readily, and stopped herself just in time from adding, "if you had I'm sure you would have done much better." For a moment she was silent as she pondered how odd it was that the same God Who had made her should make him and the furtive gipsies.

"I will be getting back to Auchendee noo," he said.

"No, don't go quite yet," she put in quickly, "for I want to ask you something. We'll sit down for a minute or two. You can sit on my seat if you like."

She seated herself on the same stump of tree where she had sat when she had brought Napier Rand to see the Loch. "Yesterday, how did you know I belonged to the manse when I had never told you?" she asked.

"I saw ye aince at the manse gate," he said, "and aifter that I heard some folk lift your name and kent wha ye were."

He mentioned this as a fact but she accepted it as a compliment. She was consumed with curiosity to know what the folk had said about her, but she could not of course ask directly and she could think of no subtle way of inquiring.

He sat, with drawn-up shoulders, gazing at her. She was quite unlike anyone he had ever seen before, she who was so obviously made for laughter and love, to be protected from life. Those eyes had never wept tempestuously or been dimmed with tears too poignant to fall, that mouth had never lamonted but merely pouted. No sad history clung to her; she had no unhappiness to pass to those around her, and he did not want any unhappiness even from those it tore his heart to part with. He was heavy with it himself, he wanted to escape from it.

Ever since that night he had lain crouched in the settle and heard the minister's voice denouncing him and Joe Stewart, he had felt he was being dogged by something which waited just behind his back, followed him everywhere he went, turned when he turned. He felt he must rid himself of it at any cost, go anywhere in the world to evade the unsleeping Evil Eye that pursued him. In Lilith Gillespie's world there were no Evil Eyes, and he belonged to her world as much as she did, it owed him everything for keeping him an exile so long. But it would be as easy to grasp the rainbow in the spray as to force his way into it. Even his very gazing at Lilith Gillespie was like midnight looking on daylight, a shadow lying in the sun.

"Why are you staring at me like that?" she asked him suddenly.

"I didna ken I was looking at ye," he replied, and moved his head away.

"What is your name?" she inquired.

"Malcolm Armit."

"And how long have you been here?"

"Aboot twa month," he answered warily.

"So have I," she sighed. Then, changing her tone, she said severely: "And do you know I have never once seen you in church all the time you have been here? I'm sure your people would be very disapproving if they knew."

"I have no people."

"Oh, but you must have," she protested; "surely you have. No father, or mother, or brothers? And where do you live at Auchendee?"

"Wi' Janet and Enoch MacDiarmid."

"And do you like living there?"

"Ay, it's as guid as maist places. I get ma meat three times a week."

"Oh."

"Ay. O' course I bargained for that afore I went."

"And what does Enoch MacDiarmid do?"

"He's a crofter."

"You mean he has animals and plant things?"

"Ay, but he's no planting any tatties this year."

"Why not?"

"Because he says he's no going to plant tatties juist for the Marquis o' Moreneck's deer that come and dig them up as though they had a grape."

"Oh, but I think that such a pity; the poor deer will starve, and they are such beautiful animals."

"They eat as muckle as a coo."

"Do they? But look how graceful they are compared to a cow."

"Ye get milk frae a coo and ye get naething frae a deer."

Neither spoke for some time until he rose, a little dazed, and said he had better be getting alang noo. She watched him making his way through the wood to the road, lifting his feet over the great tree roots which sprawled across his path. Then she listened to the rumbling of his cart until it was swallowed by the wind.

The following day was Sunday and Lilith went to church as usual with her Aunt Euphemia, who fussed so at the last moment they always just missed being late. To-day they were the last two people to enter the church, and Lilith had no sooner taken her threepenny bit from her glove and placed it safely on the ledge in front of her when Sandy Rintoul sounded the tuning-fork. As she sat there beside her aunt she became conscious that someone was watching her and her eyes stole uneasily round the church until they alighted upon Malcolm Armit in the shadows of a deep pew. Somehow the sight of him sitting there startled her violently and she felt her heart beat wildly at her side. The dark little church became suffocatingly close and her grandfather's sermon seemed so interminable she wondered desperately if it were ever going to end. She was not listening to it, only the text, "All the foundations of the earth are out of course," she heard unconsciously, for he repeated it so often it echoed through his sermon like a refrain. In her unthinking nervousness she twisted one of the buttons on her glove round and round until it came off and fell to the floor, with a noise that sounded as loud to her shocked ears as a falling cymbal. She was relieved beyond measure when at last she found herself outside again. Aunt Euphemia stopped to speak to a woman about her ill child, and while Lilith stood beside her she watched the people coming out of church, the Barnfingal congregation taking one path to the road, the Auehendee the other. But she did not see Malcolm Armit come forth and so supposed he must have left before her. She could not have told as she stood there whether she were glad or otherwise that she had not seen him again.

The silent people passed by her and she watched them pensively. Most of the Barnfingal men had weepers on their hats, for there had been a death last week, and there was so much intermarriage in the clachans that a death in one cottage usually meant a near bereavement to all. The two Barnfingal elders, like crows in their Sabbath blacks, stalked past. As they turned the bend in the path one of their low voices was borne to her.

"Wha was yon in Gow's auld pew?"

Chapter Five

AS the glow of the fire dimmed into ashiness and the loud-voiced clock wheezed off the short hours, Callum would sit alone in the silent cottage kitchen at night. His thoughts revolved in his head like a clumsy piece of machinery over which he was always trying to gain control. Usually it was the girl from the manse he ruminated over, but lately, although he saw her now nearly every day, she had lapsed from his thoughts like an accepted thing. It was Fiona who now troubled him. She was the small cog that was upsetting the whole structure of his machinery. His worried thoughts travelled round and round her, tried to evade her, blot her out of his memory, but at the back of his mind he was conscious that she was still there, too real, too importune to be overlooked. He had tried so hard to forget her he had not answered her last three letters, although he was aware as he read them that they had begun to reveal a certain restiveness. They were never long, for they took her so weary a time to write; but now she was asking him questions, and between the arrival of each letter there was a shorter period. Uneasily he waited for her to stop writing to him, which was the way he wanted to end things with her; but, after three of her letters had brought no reply, Fiona wrote a fourth, saying she was tired of the Mather household and could he not find her a situation near him?

Callum sweated when he thought of Fiona coming to Auchendee. He realized as he read her letter that he must break with her quickly, once and for all. After all, he argued to himself, he had never wanted to fall in love with her, and again there rose in him the old smouldering resentment that he had never been able to subdue her. There was no good of course merely not answering her letters, for that would make her all the more anxious, and she might appear any day walking down the road from Dormay. But he could not break with her by letter, for then he would be admitting for all to see that there had been something definite between them, something her relations might even attempt to hold him to, and it was never his policy to do anything which he could not afterwards safely deny.

The only way out was to see her and break with her in words, but this he was afraid to do in case he would not be strong enough to withstand the old unwelcome spell which had bound him to her. The very sight of her, the sound of her voice, her touch, might inflame him as they had done of old, fire his brain until he felt pantingly she was the only thing he wanted in the world. But to see her was the only way out; he must be prepared for her, fortified against her. One could do anything, move anyone, if one only concentrated on it sufficiently. Once he had come to this conclusion, he hurriedly throned it in his mind and shut out all thoughts which questioned and doubted its authority.

Fraser, the shepherd, and MacIntosh, the grieve, thought it was they who arranged for him to take a large flock of hogs to the Lowlands, but it was Callum who instilled the idea into them that he would be the best person to send. Ill-fortune attended him from the very beginning of his journey. He took every precaution to fill up the peat hags, which abounded in their wild pilgrimage over the hills, to prevent the sheep falling into them, but although he averted that danger he lost many of the flock through disease and was kept occupied skinning all the way.

On the second day, when he was many miles from Auchendee, the mist came down and shrouded him and his grey flock. He tried to proceed in spite of it, but it grew thicker and thicker, and he found he had wandered from the drove path. He lay down to wait until it rose and, his hands under his armpits to try to cull some heat, fell fast asleep. He woke an hour or so later, bewildered as to his whereabouts, and turned on one side, then the blood seemed to freeze in his veins. Below him gaped a chasm so deep it made him dizzy even to look down into it. He was lying on its very edge with only a few inches separating him from its deadly depth.

He drove the dwindled sheep to the market at Birling and from there took a coach to Middleton. He was to meet Fiona in the inn courtyard where the coaches drew up, for her mistress would not permit what was termed "followers in the kitchen." She was not waiting for him when he alighted, which upset him, for he had settled in his mind that she would be there. He walked up and down the courtyard biting his nails and looking round suspiciously every few minutes as though fearful she would take him unawares. The day was raw and cold and the wind whistling down an alley reminded him uneasily of Stonemerns.

He saw her hurrying towards him through an arch in the courtyard and the feelings that mounted in him at the sight of her almost overwhelmed him. It was not pity for her that moved him. One could feel a contemptuous pity for a pretty, delicate thing whose flushes came and went under one's gaze, but not for Fiona, who stood as stoutly as a stunted tree. No, what stirred him was that dreaded fear that he would not be strong enough to break from her, that his proximity with her would turn his resolution to water, and with this fear came the insidious thought, "Why break with her? What need is there?" He was in arms at once against that question. The need, he cried within himself, of a whole wasted life waiting to be put right. Fiona spelt poverty, obscurity, hardship. He had had these things all his life, they were what he wanted to free himself from now. It would have been different had there still been a prosperous Inchbuigh Farm and had Donald Stewart, the eldest of the three brothers, been alive, but Fiona's only heritage now was the memory of fairer days. The same circle that was drawn round him was drawn round her, that circle which separated them from other people, which attracted towards it only what was unhappy, that fated circle from which he was straining every nerve to escape.

"I couldna get awa' sooner," she explained." "If Mr. Mather's sister didna arrive juist when I was setting oot half an oor syne and have to have tea and I dinna ken whit a' to heat her up aifter her journey. I'll tak' ye to a field I ken o' whaur we can sit and no be seen."

She plodded beside him until they left the town, when she led him along a path and over a dyke to the corner of a ploughed field, where they were quite sheltered from the rising wind. He spoke very little so afraid was he of giving his words rein in case they ran away with him, but when they were seated amongst the long grasses, his knee against hers, he found he could not say to her what he wanted. He moistened his lips and opened his mouth, but instead of telling her what he had come to say he heard himself ask lamely,

"Have ye heard onything o' your hame folk?"

"Ay," she answered mournfully, "and och-hey, Callum, Joe's deid."

If she had said the, sky had fallen she could not have startled him more. Joe dead ...Joe, who was as big and strong and powerful as an oak, with his surly, handsome face which every girl from Gilhead to Naver hoped she would see looking back at her when she gazed in the mirror at midnight on Hallowe'en.

"He canna be deid," Callum said flatly, "for I saw him no so long back."

She bent forward over her folded arms in her distress.

"Och-hey, Callum, he's deid as a clod o' earth. He ne'er was himsel' syne he went doon to the Lawlands. He said he felt the air so flat he couldna fill his lungs wi' it and he couldna get his sleep at nicht. He didna settle into things at the factory like Howard and Sam did. He fretted o'er such sma' things and he didna like to be left to himsel'. The Lawlands did for him, for one day he juist laid on his back wi' his tongue oot and de'ed. Ho, he was always a bit slow, Joe, but he took no time o'er deeing."

Her voice was fraught with melancholy and she sat gazing straight before her while her mind strove to unravel the secrets of life and death. She had heard them speak of the low road, that underground road which takes the soul after death to its birthplace. When Joe's soul had left his body, had it fought and battled its way along that dark road to Inchbuigh? Had he stood with face upturned and hands outstretched to feel again the heavy mountain rain? Had the rain fallen all round him and he could not feel it? Had the wind blown over the moorlands and not stirred a hair on that phantom brow? Was he wandering even now amongst these hills where he belonged, scattered amongst which were the crofts he had known as a boy but whose apple-garths now blossomed beside ruined cottages?

Callum moved restlessly beside her. He wished she had not told him about Joe, for he had the feeling that Joe was going to haunt him, that now he would never be able to forget Mr. Cameron's words which rang in his ears like a bell of doom. Surely she must see that it would take more than the Lowlands to kill a giant like

Joe Stewart. Did she not realize that a secret something must have been dogging him, weakening his frame? His thoughts swerved like frightened birds.

He sat with his big head fallen forward, trying to build up his resolutions again. Nothing had gone as he had meant it to go. Already he was conscious of the feeling creeping over him that she had always given him at Gilhead; her very presence brought comfort to bruised senses, strength to beaten pride. There was about her the calm of a deep pool into which a waterfall tumbles, disturbing only the point of contact.

He moved uneasily at her side and again moistened his lips. His eyes wandered shiftily round to her and he saw poking up from her rough cape an unfamiliar pink wrapper with little sprigs dotted over it. He blackened his mind with the thought that he must tell her soon, before it was too late and he could not.

"Fiona."

It was out before he knew and he wondered if it sounded as unnatural to her as it did to him.

"Ay."

She did not stir, she could not expect what was coming. She sat very still amongst the grasses which were bending and whitening with the wind.

"I've been thinking it's aboot time things atween ye and me cam' to an end."

Still she did not move, gave no perceptible sign of anything untoward happening.

"Whit way?"

"Aweel…" Instead of being brutal, he sounded merely cringing, as though craving a favour he was ashamed to ask. "Aweel, Fiona, things have gone so black agin us I dinna think we will e'er be able to come thegither agin."

"Hoo?"

"That's hoo," he muttered.

"But things are no verra black," she said. "Ye've got work and are earning a wage."

"But no enow for twa to live on," he inserted quickly.

She turned and looked at him and he saw her wide mouth was lifted at one corner into a crooked half-smile. His gaze fell before hers. She was not taking it as he had expected her to take it; he could have torn himself away so much more easily from supplication and tears, even from injured, flaming pride. For the first time he felt inferior to her and this feeling made him resentful and malicious.

"Ye see I dinna feel the same to ye as I did aince," he said with calculated slowness.

"That's no it, Callum Lamont," she replied, and he felt her eyes still dwelling on him as though they were seeing into the dark places of his soul where he never dared to look. "If that was it, it would no be so bad, I would say guid-bye to ye and guid luck to ye. But ye feel the same to me as e'er ye did, and that's whit mak's it bad. Ye're doing this no because ye dinna care for me noo but because o' some ither reason. And I will tell ye something mair afore ye gang. This is the hardest thing ye have e'er done."

"It's a lee," he refuted, "it's a blasted lee," and he would have given anything at that moment to make it true.

They had risen to their feet and he had forced his eyes to meet hers. It had been sheltered behind the dyke, but now they were standing the gale whirled round their heads.

"It's the hardest thing ye will e'er do," she continued, raising her voice above the buffeting wind which caught her words immediately they left her mouth and tore with them into space. And ye think by leaving me noo ye will be rid o' me, but I tell ye ye will no. Ye'll ne'er get rid o' me, Callum Lamont, no, though ye live to the crack o' doom."

He almost ran from her into the safety of the darkening afternoon, stumbling over the unaccustomed ground. He ran from her as one would run from a witch. Once he looked back as though to reassure himself that after all it was only Fiona. She was standing on the dyke, the wind fiercely tugging at her clothes, shouting at him. His unreasonable haste increased. It seemed a long time afterwards that some of her words were borne to his ears, as though the spiteful wind had gathered them greedily to throw after him.

"Ye'll see ye'll always want me noo mair than onything else ...och-hey ...ye'll see ye'll . . ."

Chapter Six

"I WONDER what she finds to do when she goes out by herself," mused Elizabeth. "She's not the lonely, mooning type."

"She never says" said Euphemia.

"She never would," replied Alice, "she loves making mysteries. If she were going to Lowestoft she would label her trunks Folkestone. You remember, Lucy was like that too, making secrets about nothing."

"She was not nearly so pleased as I expected her to be when Mrs. Rand invited her to Edinburgh," commented Elizabeth.

"And she used to build so on that invitation," put in Euphemia. "You remember, Elizabeth, the way she used to run for the letters whenever the mail arrived."

"Yes," answered her sister, puckering her brow."She has been much more content here lately."

"Except for those last few days," said Euphemia, lowering her voice."She has hardly spoken at all since Monday, and when she has she has been quite cross."

"It's almost as though something were preying on the child's mind. I've noticed she never goes about the house singing as she used to do—like a skylark in that shaky treble."

"I can't understand it," said Elizabeth, "and I don't like it at all. It was far more like Lilith aching to go to Edinburgh than being contented in Barnfingal. I shall be relieved when she leaves to-morrow."

"Oh, but, Elizabeth," expostulated Euphemia, "what possible harm could happen to her here?"

The door was suddenly opened but no one appeared. Instead a voice said from behind it,

"Aunt Elizabeth, Bella's no more milk, so I'm going over to Davidson's Farm for another pint."

"All right, darling," murmured Elizabeth.

"If you and Bella and the pint of milk could wait two minutes while I finish this note," said Alice, "I'll come with you. I always feel cobwebby if I stay in the house all day."

There was a perceptible pause, then the voice behind the door said,

"Oh, Aunt Alice, I don't think I would come if I were you—it's so very wet underfoot," and the door shut quietly but definitely.

Her aunts' startled silence seemed to pursue Lilith as she hurried up the sodden path to the road. How unwise she had been to show so very plainly that she did not wish Aunt Alice to come with her. Now, of course, they would wonder, question amongst themselves, and she had always been so careful and clever before. Her plausibility and variety of excuses for going out on the most inclement afternoons had amazed and frightened her. Now she had ruined everything, had herself set dread suspicion on foot, but of course, she comforted herself, unless they followed her their wildest imaginings could never conceive what she did when she was out alone. And she knew they would never follow her, she always felt quite safe once she was outside; what she was afraid of was being kept in that house, of not being permitted to leave it, of unseen, unknown forces restraining her.

She told herself it was impossible, that a house was no more alive than a table or a chair, but she could not escape from the disturbing thought that the manse knew her guilty secret, knew where she went when she left it, had become disapproving and alien to her. When she tiptoed down its stairs as quietly as she could they creaked and squeaked warningly as though trying to call to her aunts; when she took the handle of its door in both hands so as to close it as gently as possible, the door was torn from her grasp and angrily slammed behind her.

She hesitated in her hurried walk, wondering if she should return for her aunt, but she reassured herself quickly that that would be a very foolish thing to do. Only she did wish now she had waited for her. He would probably not be there, as he had not been for the last four days, and if he were it would have been so splendid to have airily gone by and never looked over the bridge. But she had been so desperate to know if he would be there that she felt she could not have borne to forgo this precious opportunity of finding out, even at the risk of those stolen, furtive meetings being discovered.

Why had he not come for those last four evenings? It seemed long, empty years since she had last seen him. She could not believe it was only a few days ago that she had sat beside him and playfully traced with her finger the unyouthful lines round his grim, set mouth. What could be keeping him away?

Surely, oh, surely, he would not have left Auchendee without telling her! Perhaps he had gone away because he found he cared for her and wanted to renounce everything.... She was a little doubtful about this, but it was so gallant a thought she derived a certain painful satisfaction from it. She hurried on. Perhaps he was offended at something, he was so inclined to be resentful. Feverishly she ransacked her mind, trying to recollect anything she had said at their last meeting which he could possibly have misconstrued. Perhaps he was going to Barnfingal by the hills to avoid her. Perhaps he would never come to meet her again....

She felt sick with apprehension when she reached the bridge on the way to the farm. But he was not there. She leant against a tree, unable to go on through sheer lack of breath. Was this love? she asked herself desperately as she had asked herself a hundred times before. If it were, it was not the gay, romantic pageant she had imagined it to be before she came to the manse. Never in those care-free days, which now seemed so long ago, had she associated it with heavy footsteps and a dark, still figure who watched her intently from under brooding brows.

Her life since the evening when she had first met him had been so fraught with emotion, pitched to a key too high for her to sustain, that only now had she learnt what exhaustion was. Its heights of ecstasy made her dizzy, and in moments when she was alone she had trembled at its hidden depths, while her whole being was as though rent with vague longings, forebodings and untrammelled desire.

She was dismayed and terrified at the revelation of the emotions which dwelt, hitherto unknown, within her, became panic-stricken when she realized how all her days were now spent counting off the minutes until she should see him, told herself weakly that this was the last time she would go, the very last time, knew with frightening penetration that it was not.

She set out from the farm as quickly as possible in case he came and went before she could reach the bridge. Then she was angry with herself when she discovered the way her thoughts were tending. She slackened her pace and told herself emphatically that really it did not matter a whit to her whether he were there or not; to prove it she would march by and never once look over. But the temptation was too strong. Miserably she knew she could no longer keep up pretences with herself. Her footsteps flagged until they stopped altogether at the bridge. She would take one lightning peep before passing on, only for interest's sake, to see if he were standing below, waiting for her like the dark geni of the pool.

A movement behind her made her start so violently that some milk splashed out of the jug. Startled, she looked round to see him watching her from the other side of the road. Tears of mortification sprang to her eyes and threatened to overflow.

"Why did you frighten me so?" she demanded, her breath coming short and quick. "I was looking to see if there were any trout in the burn."

She knew the muddled lie merely emphasized her act. Of course she should have taken no notice that he had caught her leaning over the bridge. What she did had nothing to do with him. Oh, why had she not allowed Aunt Alice to come with her and then all this would have been saved?

"I didna mean to frichten ye," he said. "I was only coming alang the road wunnering if ye would be here. Are ye coming to the mill? I'll tak' your jug for ye."

In spite of herself his words eased her, as they were meant to do, for they gave her an opportunity to taunt him.

"Oh no," she said haughtily, "why should I come to the mill?" and very coldly she looked through him, her chin raised high in the air.

He forbore to remind her that that was where they had gone on their last few meetings.

"I had something to say to ye. Ye see, I have no seen ye noo for some days."

She was very surprised at this announcement. "Indeed? Haven't you? I'm afraid I cannot say I had noticed...."

"I had to tak' some sheep to Birling."

So that was it. She nearly burst into tears with disappointment. He had not gone away because he was afraid of his love for her, but only because of some provoking sheep that had to be driven to the Lowlands. The uneasy thought intruded itself upon her that he had not told her he would be absent on purpose to keep her in suspense.

"I only came out for some milk," she said, holding out the flowered jug to prove her words." And I am going home now and shall bid you good-bye, for it is unlikely I shall ever see you again. I travel to Edinburgh to-morrow to stay for ever and ever."

She did not expect her words to have the effect upon him that they had. He crimsoned darkly under his swarthiness, his alarmed eyes gazed at her as though he could not believe what she had said, his hands opened and shut.

"Well, perhaps not for ever," she said, relenting.

"Ye will come back," he said, the words strangling in his throat. "Say to me ye will come back."

"Perhaps," she answered, not looking at him, her head turned to one side.

"I will be waiting for ye," he said, stepping nearer. "It's for ye I'm biding noo. Swear to me that ye'll come back."

"Perhaps," she repeated, whispering it this time and moving away from him.

"Lilith," he said urgently, and her name sounded magical and unfamiliar on his lips, "dinna gang hame juist noo. Come to the mill syne it's the last time I'll see ye afore ye gang."

"It's muddy," she said faintly.

"I'll see ye dinna get your feet muddy," he promised.

"I came out for milk," she lipped. "Bella will be waiting."

"She can wait."

After all she was not going to see him again for weeks, perhaps a month. Her tottering defences fell and she allowed him to unclasp her hot fingers on the jug. He hid it behind a boulder and helped her to descend the precipitous bank. The wind whipped at a bush and they were sprayed with raindrops. He led her to the disused mill, which creaked and groaned at their every step as though resenting their intrusion. It was a dusty, ghostly place, with death-ticks beating in its rotten walls, ridden with mice and overrun with skuttling spiders and giant beetles. But Lilith had never been conscious of these things until to-day. Before, with her hand safe in his, and her eyes shining, she had liked to listen to the way in this dust-muffled place their whispered voices echoed windily and hollowly, like the voices of supernatural beings.

But to-night, as she sat tense and tremulous, she almost wished she had not come. Somehow she seemed so very far away from the Lilith who set out from the manse only a short half-hour ago. At the slightest sound she jumped involuntarily and he had to reassure her. Dubiously she looked up at him, but his face was shadowed completely in the darkened, low-roofed loft. He was so close to her, like a mountain, that she felt stifled.

"When ye are in Edinburgh ye will no forget—say ye will no forget."

She opened her mouth to speak, but her throat was so dry no words came. He bent towards her and her heart contracted, but she could not have told what emotion it was that stirred it.

Book Four

Chapter One

ALICE entered the room her niece shared with her to find it strewn with clothes of all description, while an empty trunk stood in one corner. A very flushed Lilith was pulling out the difficult drawers of the chest and pushing them, shudderingly protesting, back again.

"Good heavens, Lilith," expostulated her aunt, "you haven't packed a thing."

"I know I haven't," answered Lilith, pressing the back of her hand to her brow and sitting down suddenly on the lumpy bed.

"You'll need to waken up," said Alice. "We leave at cockcrow to-morrow."

"I know we do," replied Lilith, looking hopelessly round the room.

"I'll help you," her aunt said generously. "You hand me things and I'll fold them and put them in. I may not be good at much in this world, but I am a good packer. We'll put in all your heavy things first. Why, what a beautiful dress."

"Papa gave me it for my seventeenth birthday," Lilith said listlessly.

"And slippers and stockings and even a handkerchief to match!" exclaimed Alice. "That's so like Glen, he always did do things handsomely. You should look lovely in this, Lilith. Put it on and let me see you in it."

A movement behind them made them both look round. It was Aunt Euphemia standing in the doorway, watching them. She entered the untidy room and sat on a chair while Alice dressed her niece in the pale rose satin frock. Lilith's animation returned to her as she drew on her best clocked stockings and put her feet into the tiny, pointed slippers.

"You look like someone who has stepped out of a frame," declared Alice. "Come, and I'll do your hair and then you must run down and let Aunt Elizabeth see you. Tell her from me that you are the Gillespies' Last Hope. She *does* look pretty, doesn't she, Euphemia?" she demanded of her sister, irritated by her continued silence.

"Yes," acquiesced Euphemia, "but of course she won't be able to wear that dress yet."

"Why not?"

"Well, it's coloured and it's not twelve months since poor Glen died."

"Good heavens, don't be ridiculous, Euphie; Mrs. Rand is not going to have it counted out to the day. Wear it as much as ever you can, Lilith. I don't believe in keeping things; opportunity never waits. There now! Don't shake your head too much as it's more faith than pins that is keeping up your hair. Now, come and we'll let Aunt Elizabeth see you."

When she was left alone Euphemia continued to sit stiffly in her chair, her hands folded tightly in her lap. She had not nearly enough to think about and her unemployed thoughts were in the habit of straying to morbid pastures. A deep resentment had taken possession of her in spite of herself. She felt suddenly passionately jealous of Lilith, or, rather, of the expectant youth her little niece embodied. Her pretty frocks and lace-edged petticoats, her ribboned hats and fur-trimmed cape, which lay in disorder about the room, seemed to be taunting her. She felt old and colourless, a flower that had never bloomed, a tree that had never blossomed. Everything was done for Lilith, she was given every chance: was standing, her hands full, on the very threshold of life. Her roads would not all end in blind alleys as her aunt's had done. Euphemia's tongue clucked in her mouth and she swallowed painfully in her long, thin throat.

It was ten o'clock before Lilith's trunk was packed. Bella strapped it for her and swore nothing would make her forget to "chap" her at six o'clock next morning. Lilith listened to the old maid's footsteps going noisily downstairs. At last she was alone. She told herself she would undress very hurriedly and climb into bed and pretend to be asleep when Aunt Alice came in. But she went on standing in the middle of the floor as though unable to move, clutching at the neck of her petticoat, her eyes staring widely at the wall. Then she was seized by the frantic desire to see him, to hear him reassure her, to be made to feel that she could lean on him. So strong was the desire that she wanted to run out that very night, at that very moment, to find him, not to stop running, not to think of anything, until she found him....

A knock sounded at the door. She started, every nerve on edge. She did not respond but looked over her shoulder to see whom it was. For one wild, frenzied moment her distended eyes expected to see him stand in the doorway.

It was Aunt Euphemia who entered with a purple silken scarf in her hands. She thought it might be of some use to Lilith—no, no, it was not good of her at all. She would never wear it now and Lilith might as well have it. She did so hope her niece would sleep well and be refreshed for to-morrow's journey; she herself was going to rise early to be sure that she got safely away. Lilith told her wearily that she must not think of troubling, but Aunt Euphemia said insistently that she certainly would. At the door she paused and looked round. "Lilith, dear," she said, "no matter what your Aunt Alice says, I wouldn't wear that dress. Mrs. Rand will think no more of you if you do." When the door shut behind her, Lilith began to undress. Everything was sordid and jaded. She felt if she saw her aunt appear again in the doorway something in her, taut to breaking-point, would snap.

She climbed into bed, turning her face to the wall. As passionately as she had longed for Aunt Euphemia to leave her, she longed now for Aunt Alice to come to bed, be near, talk to her until she fell asleep. She must not think. She told herself urgently that on no account must she think.

Early next morning Alice and her niece left the manse for Edinburgh. It was a still, grey day with mist hanging like ghosts from the trees. The sodden air was heavy and Lilith had the stifling feeling that everything would wait exactly as it was for her return.

The stir and bustle of the towns through which they passed bewildered her after the solitude and quietness of Barnfingal. She never could recollect afterwards anything about her arrival at Mrs. Rand's or her first impression of her hostess. All she was aware of was that the lofty apartments of the house in Martin Square seemed swallowingly large, probably because she had grown so accustomed to the manse's bare rooms with their sloping ceilings. Here her voice sounded unfamiliar while other people's seemed equally strange, as though coming from a far distance.

There was an unreal calm about this new, sheltered existence after the last pent-up, stressful months, and she felt as one lost in a dream. It was like a backwater compared to that black, bottomless pool whose hidden, swirling eddies had so dangerously fascinated her. But as the days glided by, the feeling of unreality fell from her. It was as though she were awake now and had dreamed that other life. Surely, surely it must all have been a dream. Childishly she willed it all to have been a dream.

This was a life she could understand, she could comprehend the people around her. No longer did she feel in a wilderness bounded by howling winds and the roots of trees. Life here was lived by the unhurried ticking of the clock, not by windy seasons and the weak rays of the sun. There were no stealthily-creeping mists, no desolation of moorland, no troubled Loch. The trees in the Square garden were pruned and enclosed by railings; they did not throw wild shadows and toss their arms as though possessed.

There was so much to do, the days were so happily full, that one had little time to think of what was past. But sometimes at five o'clock in the afternoon one would uneasily wonder if heavy footsteps were passing along a certain road, if they halted on a humped bridge and then passed on....Sometimes when one gazed at the placid, unlined countenance of Mrs. Rand one asked oneself what she would say and think if her calm eyes could see into the hidden places of one's mind; and when one caught Napier Rand looking at one in his quick, keen way, one's heart seemed almost to stop beating.

It was more difficult to become intimate with him than it was with his delightful mother.

His temperament was both aloof and exacting. Even in his most youthful days he had been neither ardent nor eager; he was rarely stirred and never excited. He deplored it but had to acknowledge that life left him on the whole quite cold. His smile was rare and seldom spontaneous, as though it had appeared only on second thoughts.

Lilith thought him quite the handsomest man she had ever seen, even handsomer in a less spectacular way than her magnificent-looking father. There was not an irregularity in Rand's good-looking features except a small mole, like a mistake, at the corner of one of his eyes, which lent his face an expression of oddity. He was commandingly tall. Lilith was tremulous and shy in his presence, but once or twice she had the impression that he liked to be beside her. This intangible knowledge seemed to illumine her whole being, filled her with a radiancy which must surely have shone from her face. At other times she feared desperately he must find her very stupid, but alone in her room, after she had seen him, she never covered her face with her hands or bit at her lip or wished passionately she were different.

Chapter Two

THE more dismal the wintry weather, the brighter by contrast were the softly-lit rooms of the house in Martin Square. Outside snow caked the railings of the Square gardens and the uppermost branches of the trees. Wheels of coaches and carriages were scarcely audible and footsteps became padded. The white flakes eddied down, lighter than air, blown hither and thither on no breath of wind. The snow lost its first unsullied freshness, became hardened with footsteps and rutted with wheels. The falling of heavy rain drove one's mind unwillingly to a silent manse. It made the leafless branches of the trees glisten, polished the railings and coursed in mimic burns down the gutters. Not a note was heard from the unseen town birds.

Mrs. Rand had invited Lilith to stay with them for a month, but her visit was lengthened into several, until it became difficult for Napier to imagine what the house had been without her. That he, thrown into such close proximity, became attracted by her was almost inevitable. There was something appealing in her timidity, something wistful in her prettiness, while everything about her, the delicacy of her skin, the fineness of her hair, her fluttering little hands and tiny feet, satisfied his fastidious taste. She was so unspoiled by sophistication, so aglow with youth, that she came into his tired life like a spring wind into a room where the curtains had always been drawn. He liked to watch her little face light up eagerly, liked to see her eyes shine and her cheeks bright. It never struck him there was something feverish about her spirits, he never suspected any shadow lying behind those shining eyes, or considered she was flushed with anything but vivacity. Sometimes, to be sure, he caught her gazing at him almost questioningly, and only the presence of his mother debarred him from crossing the room and kissing those parted lips.

Unconsciously Mrs. Rand stiffened in her attitude to her guest. The strongest emotion she had ever had was her love for her son, and she knew perfectly well what he was thinking as he leant back in his chair while he watched her goddaughter's small, bent head.

She became appreciably less delightful than she had been at the beginning of Lilith's visit.

Lilith was quick to feel the difference. She trembled as she realized how very near she had been once or twice to making a confidante of Mrs. Rand. Now, as her godmother became colder to her, she seemed to Lilith to change into quite another person. She saw that behind that untroubled countenance there lay harshness, that those calm grey eyes lacked understanding. Because she had never had any temptations she considered herself invulnerable. She would be hard in her judgments, stern in her denouncements, implacable in her decisions.

No longer could Lilith shut her eyes to what was happening. She had thrust the knowledge to the very back of her mind, she had tried to crowd it out of her life, she had told herself it was not, could not be true. She wrapped it in swaddling clothes and left it while she tried to muster sufficient strength to face it, but at last recognition was inevitable. Each night she paced her carpeted bedroom floor in her stocking-soles; her fingers became drenched with tears; she wrung her hands in despair, but her pacings led to no decision, her tears and wringing of hands solved nothing.

She had no one to tell, no one to whom she could turn. Oh, surely in this wide world there was someone who would understand, who would help her, comfort her. She dare not tell her godmother. Her eyes searched Napier Rand's fine face. Would she find coldness and incomprehension there as she had found it in his mother's? She could not say, she did not know, everyone was a closed book to her, written in an unfamiliar language. And every day brought fresh fears. Every clock was mercilessly ticking off the moments, the pressing, urgent, insistent moments that no tears, no heart-breaking prayers could stay.

She wrote to the manse and told her aunts that she thought she ought to return now. Would Aunt Euphemia be so kind as to write and tell her so, making some excuse? She waited, sick at heart, for the letter to come. It arrived within a week and Mrs. Rand was duly told that Aunt Euphemia had written asking her to return as Aunt Elizabeth was not so well.

The excuse sounded flimsy and vague to Napier. He suspected Lilith had not been happy lately and he connected this unhappiness with his mother's changed attitude towards her. He was annoyed and angry with the unreasonableness of his mother, but it was not until he heard Lilith was going that he realized how much she had become a part of his life. He could not tell whether she cared for him or not, he was afraid she must find him old and staid. For the first time for many years he wanted to do something in a hurry, but he could scarcely propose to her in his own house, particularly when his mother, if Lilith's answer did happen to be in the affirmative, would be so resentful. He asked himself irritably why it was parents seemed to be under the impression that one's store of love was limited and that when one fell in love with a woman one drew from the reserve set aside for them. Now he would have to wait until Lilith went back to Barnfingal and travel there soon after himself.

He bade her good-bye, holding her hand longer than was necessary in his firm grasp and gazing down into the depths of her eyes. She heard him say he would like to come to see her at the manse if she would permit it. She had slept badly the previous night and was keyed to such a state of nervous apprehension that she did not know what she answered. She told herself all the journey home, her misery dulled into a hollow aching, that she had been so ungracious he would never come now.

Her grandfather met her at Davar as he had met her nearly a year ago when she had travelled from London, only then it had been the height of summer. Now snow lay on the distant hills and only some of the trees showed a hint of the spring which came so late to the district and which made so short a stay. Oh, when the bright, plumed offspring of the chestnut had spread into five-fingered leaves, when the sticky, pointed shoots and little buds like crumpled wings had burst into foliage, where would she be? What would have happened to her? So weary was she that she prayed she would be dead, not as she used to picture when she heard music played and saw herself, lovely with death, surrounded by weeping friends; but dead and forgotten, away from everyone, with the earth heaped so heavily on top of her that no sound, no voice, no feeling could reach her.

They drove along the country road beside the Loch, through silent woods and over little brawling burns. It was all so sad and old. The hills were scarred. The pines and heather, burnt a bright rust-brown by the late frost, were more reminiscent of autumn than of spring. The boles of the trees which bore tender shoots were streaked with green or covered thickly with grey lichen. From the mould of last year's leaves primroses pushed pale heads amongst the far-reaching roots of the gaunt trees. Little white lambs gambolled weakly on their black hind legs, but their very youth and whiteness only served to contrast the greyness of the old sheep at whose sides they lay or gambolled.

Nearer and nearer they drew to the manse. Someone, perhaps even he, had brought a cartload of hay along the road on a windy day, for netted hay was caught over some broom bushes like a cage and a piece of it, like a waif's hand, dangled from a tree.

After all the greetings had been said, Lilith went to her room. As she climbed the wooden stairs she once more had the curious feeling that despite its atmosphere of damp stagnation this house was alive, could see, hear, listen, wait, could breathe, had a heart that beat, that felt the shame, the sacrifices, the weaknesses of those who lived in it.

She did not know whether she were relieved or not that Aunt Alice was not at home and she had the bedroom to herself. On the flounced cloth of the dressing-table lay some books which her grandfather had come across and thought she might like. They were old-fashioned, for they had belonged to her father and aunts when they were young. Tears pricked her eyes as she looked inside the thin volumes at the square, lined pictures depicting fringed, foreshortened children at work and play.

Before she took off her cape and bonnet she knelt down at the bedside, her hands clasped, in an effort to relieve her mind by praying to God, but her thoughts would not assemble, no words would come. She had prayed so wildly before to Him not to make it true; she had beseeched her own father wherever he was in the Outer World to save her, but nothing had happened, no unspoken answer had come to her prayers. Now she found she could not pray even brokenly. Then gradually her thoughts began to move as they had never, like unknown soldiers grimly martialling at dawn to carry out an execution. She knelt stiff and very upright, her hands unclasped and fell to her sides, her frail face, framed in the pretty bonnet, gazed rigidly at the wall before her.

She had brought this upon herself by her own unlicensed wickedness; he was to blame too, equally as much as she, but no more. She would have to suffer for her wickedness; that was why God was not answering her prayers, why her father could not hear. Not if she prayed to the clap of doom would she free herself from the sin she had committed. Suffering did not blot out wickedness. No miracle was going to happen.

What could she do? What, she asked herself dumbly, her lips moving, was the "rightest" thing she could do now? Marry him? She must not think of herself, she must think of what was best for her unborn child. Yes, she supposed drearily that marrying him was the only thing she could do now.

And Napier Rand? She shuddered suddenly and violently from head to foot and, covering her face with her hands, sat on the floor. Oh, why had this thing happened to her? What baleful influence had been at work marring, spoiling, ruining for all time what was fairest and purest?

She wondered if Napier Rand would come to Barnfingal. A paroxysm of shivering seized her and her teeth chattered. She determined to say nothing to anyone for a week, in which she would wait to see if he would come. If he did not, she would have to tell someone, Aunt Elizabeth, perhaps ...she would have to see Malcolm Armit. But if Napier Rand came she would tell him. Her hands fell folded in her lap. She would tell him everything, she would not spare herself, she would leave what was to happen to her with him. She could do no more.

Perhaps he would understand, but she supposed it would be a hard thing for another man to understand. Yet if he were in her place and she in his, she felt that now she would have understood. She felt there was no felony on earth so bad that she could not forgive it if she knew he who had committed it had suffered as she was suffering.

Chapter Three

THE quietness in the manse at night was quite different to the quietness in the big house in Martin Square. There it had been a deathly, unbroken silence which had mounted up after midnight and pressed itself like a mighty pulse against her throbbing ears. Now as she lay awake the manse seemed to come perceptibly alive with stealthy creaks and tiptoeing sounds and little hurried tickings. The wind, pressing round the house, was piteous at night, and her tired mind would will that morning would come soon, soon, lighten the square of window, make familiar the room. Her very exhaustion chased sleep farther away.

They heard from Napier Rand that he would visit them on Friday. It dawned so grey and wet Aunt Euphemia wondered if he would continue on his journey, but Aunt Elizabeth was sure he would. He arrived about noon. He seemed to Lilith to be sterner than she had imagined, but perhaps what she had to tell him threw a chill over him in her eyes, drained the warmth from his greeting. When they were alone together she impressed upon herself that she must keep very calm—he was the type of man who hated scenes and would be scared by hysterics.

He was so nervous himself that he did not notice how nervous she was, or see how tensely her hands were clasped together. He pulled at the curtains, he rubbed the floor with the point of his boot, he remarked at least four times how wet it was, and he never realized she made no response. He stood, tall, broad and upright, his hands behind his back and his back towards the room. Then he wheeled round with such suddenness to face her that she almost fainted.

"Miss Gillespie," he said, and his voice sounding husky, he quickly cleared his throat, "Miss Gillespie, I want you to know why I have come. It is to—to ask you if you—if you——" Where the devil had all his words flown?

"Yes," she said quietly, "I know why you have come."

"And will you?" he asked eagerly.

"I—I can't," she whispered. "At least," she said, lifting up her face to his, "it's not for me to say now."

"Not for you? You mean I should have spoken to your grandfather first? But 'pon my soul, I always thought that a stupid arrangement. After all it is you who would marry me, not your grandfather, so it is you, not he, who has the right to say yes or no."

"No, I don't mean that."

He looked down at her awkwardly and for the first time noticed her face was strained and white.

"Well, what do you mean, then?"

"I mean you wouldn't want to marry me perhaps if you knew everything about me."

"Why," he said, playfully chiding, "what could possibly prevent me?"

"Do you remember," she asked with difficulty, "when you came here before?"

"Yes, of course I remember."

"And it was some months after that before I came to Edinburgh."

"Yes, yes," he acquiesced. He spoke a little irritably, for he had always been annoyed with himself that he had not persuaded his mother to invite her godchild sooner, as he had intended when he left the manse.

"I—well—I," she said painfully, and he saw her white face was now streaked with red patches, "I—it was during that time that something happened."

"Something happened?" he interrogated unhelpfully. Good God, what on earth could have happened to make her look like that?

"Yes, I—I met someone."

"Ah, I see."

He had stiffened at once, in spite of himself his voice was icy.

"No, no, you don't," she cried, "you are thinking mistakenly. I—I don't love him. It's you I love, only you, but oh, don't you see? Won't you understand?"

"I'm afraid I don't," he replied definitely, "unless you are trying to tell me you had a kind of engagement with this man."

"It—it wasn't so simple as that," she said, moistening her dry lips, her eyes avoiding his.

He seemed very big standing before her in the small room, and although he was so near he seemed very far away. She could not think clearly, her thoughts refused to link up,connect. She wondered faintly where she was going to get enough air for her next breath. Oh, surely she would not have to tell him, surely, surely he would understand now; a woman would, but men were so different from women.

"I do not follow," he said in the same voice he would have used to a client he considered unnecessarily obtuse.

She felt cornered, trapped, breathless. Then with an effort she pulled herself together and, with the calmness of despair, said unevenly,

"I—I met this other man. We used to meet nearly every evening and—and on the night before I came to Edinburgh something happened. I am going to have a child."

He understood now. She heard the clock's rapid ticking and the rain dripping from the trees outside. She was conscious of his thunderstruck silence, which hung in the room like a cloud, making the air heavy and momentous. She felt his deepset eyes piercing down at her, trying to fathom her, trying to believe what she had said, then building up quite another picture of her. She moved in her chair in an effort to escape from those eyes which pinned her to it.

"This other man," he said at last, "will he marry you?"

"Yes," she answered, "I think he would if—if I asked him."

From his formal voice she knew her death-knell had sounded, but, in a stupendous effort to make herself clear, in her painful anxiety not to give a wrong impression, she made one final, desperate rally.

"But," she said, having difficulty in moving her white lips, "I don't love him. It's you I love."

He was at the door when he felt her hands put over his, staying him. It was only afterwards he realized that they had been coldly moist. He looked down into her upturned, sharpened face.

"Napier," she said, "don't go away like that, don't look at me like that. I—I don't want you to do anything—don't think I am asking you for—for anything—only when you think of me try to forget what I have told you, try to—to think of me as you thought of me before today."

She heard him go and listened until his footsteps disappeared into silence. She had thought that perhaps his love for her might be so strong he would have gone on loving her in spite of everything, but love was not strong enough to stand so harsh a blow. She had expected too much. She swayed a little on her feet as though she had stood too long.

Chapter Four

THAT evening she wrote Malcolm Armit a note which ran, "I shall be at the mill to-morrow at five o'clock." She gave it to the road-man to take to him, explaining that Bella wanted the carter to do something for her. She doubted if the road-man believed her, but she had reached that point when she did not care whether her actions were suspicious or not.

The following afternoon she set out by herself for the mill. She found it difficult to clamber down the precipitous, overgrown bank when there was no strong hand to aid her. She was the first to arrive at their destination and stood waiting for him in the dusky, ill-lit place. Listening, every nerve on edge, for the first sound to warn her of his nearness, she imagined she heard him many times before he really came.

His footsteps were inaudible on the soft ground outside and she only heard his approach when he began to climb the broken stairs. She started convulsively and her heart leapt. He seemed to sway the whole building, which groaned as though riven. His head appeared in the aperture, then his body, and she saw his eyes peer round the darkened loft to see if she were there, saw them pick her out as she stood leaning against the wall. He lifted his legs over the wooden partition and came and stood before her.

"So ye've come back," he said at last.

"Yes," she answered, "I had to return because of you."

He put out his hand to touch her, but she recoiled.

"I didn't want to come back," she cried fiercely; "it wasn't because I wanted to that I've come back. What I said was that I had to return. It's because I can't help it. I am going to have a child." She felt suddenly violently sick."And now," she said, turning on him, "what are you going to do? You have done your worst and are responsible as much as I."

"The only thing is to get marrit," he said quiet and low.

"'The only thing' — 'the only thing,'" she mimicked, beside herself. "And do you think I want to marry you? Do you imagine for one moment that I love you? I tell you, if you touch me now, if you put a finger near me, I shall scream."

He went and sat on the wooden partition which formed the door and where she saw his massive head and shoulders blocked out against the stairway's dusty light.

"I'll no come near ye," he replied sullenly. "I dinna want to touch ye. Ye say ye dinna lo'e me noo, but ye maun have aince or ye would no have met me a' yon times and let me touch ye then. Ye didna need to meet me unless ye wanted to."

"I was mad," she said huskily. "I must have been mad."

"Ye were eether mad then and sane noo, or sane then and mad noo," he commented, "but that's no here or there."

"What is here and there," she said, her breath shaking with sobs, "is that I can scarcely bear to look at you."

"Weel, dinna look at me, then. Ye dinna need to marry me if ye dinna want to. Besides," he added, feeling his ground, "I ne'er said I would marry ye."

"You will have to, you will have to," she cried tempestuously, betraying herself in her distraughtness. "You have led me into this and shall have to help me out. Think if it were born——"

"But ye say ye canna bear to look at me."

"I shall have to put up with you for its sake. I shall have to bear you because of it. Do you think if there was another way out I would not have taken it? Do you not know that I would rather do anything than marry you?"

"There was a time ye didna shudder if I touched ye."

"Don't dare remind me of that."

"And dinna ye dare staund there and gie me high, prood words. Ye're no better than me for a' your fine ways."

"I never said I was. I know I am to blame as well as you, but you are to blame more than I. You are older than I, you knew more than I did, you—took advantage of my foolishness. And now I'll have to suffer, have to marry you, when I know you are lower than the earth."

"And hoo do ye ken I am lower than the earth?"

"Because I can use my eyes and ears."

"And whit would ye say if ye larnt I was as guid as ye? Whit would ye say if ye larnt that for a' your graund ways the same blood as went through your veins went through mine?"

"I don't know what you mean."

"I mean if I am lower than the earth, so maun ye be, for there's naething to choose atween us. I belang to your family as muckle as ye do."

"I don't know what you mean."

"When ye gang back to the manse to-night, ye ask your Aunt Euphemia if she minds a place ca'ed Stonemerns. When she says 'Ay,' ye ask her if she minds a Betsy Gaughan and an Annie Lamont wha bided there. And when she says 'Ay, ay,' ye ask her whit happened to the son she left o'er twenty year back wi' Betsy Gaughan and Annie Lamont."

"What does that mean?"

"It means the son your Aunt Euphemia had at Stonemerns o'er twenty year syne was me."

"You?"

"Ay, me."

"Of course Aunt Euphemia has no children."

"Ay, she had one, and it's me."

"I don't believe you."

"Your Aunt Euphemia will tell ye if I gie ye the lee or no."

There was a pause as her stupefied brain tried to grasp what he had told her. Then she said breathlessly, as one aware of using the last chance of escape,

"Aunt Euphemia did not know you when she saw you passing on the road last year."

"It's no likely she would ken me when she hasna clappit e'en on me syne I was born."

There was another pause. Her dazed mind reeled, gaped, rocked, while her thoughts flew in fragments. Only one sentence remained whole, spoken in her grandfather's voice from a great height, "All the foundations of the earth are out of course." Why had he said those words? Why did anyone trouble to utter anything? What did anything matter in a world that was shaken to its roots? What did anything matter when you and this man were the only two people left on it, facing each other, eternity between you?

In that moment of silence, when Lilith Gillespie stood in the mill loft and gazed across at him through the faint stour of other years' gristings, she reached a pinnacle of weary resignation, touched a depth of resistless sorrow, she was never in the rest of her lifetime to reach or touch again.

He heard her sigh unbrokenly, the sigh of one who returns from unconsciousness; then he heard her voice coming monotonously to him as though from someone who, after long strife, had suddenly given in.

"And you knew—you knew all the time we were meeting that I—I was your cousin and you never told me."

"Na, I didna tell ye."

"Why not?"

"I was waiting a wee."

"For your own base ends."

She brushed past him down the creaking stairs, her dipping skirts catching dust and cobwebs. He followed her trailing footsteps and the mill was left to its own silence. When they had been speaking together their heightened voices had startled echoes from different parts of the building. Now the echoes receded, the dust they had raised settled, and the place was as it had been before they entered.

Chapter Five

"I HAVE a right to know whom his father was. I insist upon knowing—you will have to tell me."

"Darling, I would tell you if it would do any good, but that is all over and done with now."

"All over and done with! How can you say such a thing when the son you have hardly ever seen is walking the earth? I must know whom his father was, I tell you I must know."

"But I can't tell you, Lilith, it was as much his secret as mine. He was no one of very much importance—probably he died long ago."

"He must have been someone very low," said Lilith, bitter and aged with suffering, "a gipsy probably."

"Lilith!"

"He looks as though he had had a gipsy for a father."

"Lilith, how dare you say such things."

"Because if he were anyone better than the lowest you would tell me whom he was. But when you see your son you won't be able to evade him as you have evaded me, he will have no mercy upon you."

"There is no necessity whatever for me to see him, I shall refuse to see him."

"Afraid to meet your own son," said Lilith, her reddened eyes narrowed, her swollen lips sneering. "But what about Grandpapa— he will want to know, he will make you tell."

"You mustn't tell your Grandfather anything. It would kill him to know and after all those years it would be so useless. Elizabeth, she mustn't tell him, must she? You tell her she mustn't."

"But he will need to know about me."

"Not necessarily. You—you can go away somewhere."

"Yes?"

"And then—and then come back of course."

"Yes?"

"Well, he need never know—nobody need ever know."

"And what is to happen to the child when I return?"

"It can stay somewhere, there are countless places."

Lilith lifted her face from her hands and looked at her.

"Where it can grow up like him, bad and black and twisted? But it won't be as simple as that. We won't get rid of Malcolm Armit as easily as you got rid of his gipsy father."

"You can go away, he will never be able to trace you, we won't tell him where you are."

"And I could never return then—could I?— for he would still be here. And he could expose you and me. Your pretty son will stop at nothing. I know him now, I can see now how all this time he has been working for this, leading up to this. He's worse than the worst thing one can imagine. And it's because of you he is what he is. It wasn't his fault he was born—you must admit that. You had him and never stood by him, you abandoned him and let him strive for himself. You left him and he grew up like that and you didn't care. He went to a farm as herd, and now he is a carter, and you didn't care. Anything could have happened to him, but it is only when you think he is going to interfere with you that you tremble. He is wrongful and beastly but you are ten times worse."

"Lilith, Lilith, how dare you say such things. Think of Aunt Elizabeth—how bad it is for her to hear you."

"You are ten times worse I say, you are ten times worse. Do you think if this had happened to me with any other man you would have had pity? I tell you you would not. You would have been shocked and horrified and condemnatory. But you will be held responsible for what he is. You won't, you say, but one day you will have to answer for him."

"I have nothing to do with him now," said Euphemia. "I cannot help what he has done to you. That has nothing to do with me."

"It has everything to do with you," said Lilith, still in the same low, intent, unnatural voice. "But there is no good saying anything more to you for you are quite dead. Every time you wouldn't think of him, every step you took away from him, you died a little more, and the thing that lived instead of you is him. It's you who have strengthened him in his wickedness and remorselessness."

"You must be out of your mind to say such things. How can I possibly be dead when I am still alive, talking to you?"

"And now you dare to say that I can leave my child, hide it away, let it grow up like him—"

"I was only trying to help you, I didn't know you wanted it."

"Wanted it? Wanted it! Wanted what has ruined my life, my all? But don't you see, you madwoman, that it is my fault, as it was your fault, and I shall have to bear the consequences as one day you shall have to bear them. You will carry him into the next world on your back."

"But, Lilith——"

"Don't call me by name, never, never let me hear you say my name again. I tell you it's flesh and blood you would have me run away from, not——"

She had stared at her aunt's face so long that it seemed to lose all contour, now shakily dwindled, now crookedly expanded, eventually swam as though distorted by water before her aching eyes.

It was Bella who helped the fainting Lilith upstairs, who chafed her bloodless hands with her own roughened ones, who undid her buttons and tapes and put her to bed. And as Lilith saw bending over her that old face, wizened and puckered like an apple left in a loft, it seemed to her the noblest face in the world—Bella who, no matter what you did, would never look at you with changed eyes, who knew how overwhelmingly the odds had been against you, who never muttered against you but only against the bitter, hard fate that had caught you in its wheel.

When at last she fell into a fitful, restless sleep, Bella went downstairs into the kitchen where the tall jugs, with their spouts all facing in the one direction as though they had marching orders, were ready for to-morrow's milk. The candle had collapsed with the heat of the kitchen and lay curving along the table like a thick, insinuating, white worm.

She moved from the fire to the table and from the table to the many-shelved dresser, putting the kitchen to rights for the night. Then, as was her custom for five minutes before going to bed, she sat down on the wooden chair at the hearth-side. Her ears were always so full of noises that it was difficult for her to tell what she really heard and what was merely going on in her head. Usually it was at this time she heard most sounds, pattering footsteps in the lobby outside or in some dim lobby of her brain, little gusts of laughter, small, soft voices ...

But to-night she heard none of these although she sat there until late, as though she had forgotten all about herself, her head fallen forward on her bunched-up chest. When she started from her chair the house was in darkness and she had gone very cold. Stiffly she made her way through the dark across the familiar kitchen to the door, where she paused.

On every stair, on every plank, in every room of the house, she heard footsteps, and it seemed as she listened that she could distinguish one from the other : Mrs. Gillespie's heavy tread; the minister's uneven walk; Master Glen, shaking the whole house "rugging at" the bannisters, in the manner his papa was telling him so repeatedly not to do, as he ran downstairs late for breakfast; Miss Alice dancing and buoyant, never twice the same; Miss Euphemia tripping in one unbuttoned shoe; Miss Elizabeth too light, too light....

Muttering, the old maid creaked up the stairs, shaking her head every few steps as though annoyed by moths.

Malcolm Armit received a summons to the manse on the following day, which was earlier than he had expected. He was shown first of all into a room where a frail-looking woman lay on a couch. She told him that Lilith's grandfather would see him but that on no account must he tell him whom he was, for he had received so great a shock about her niece he could stand no more. Callum was quite prepared not to mention his mother's identity at present as it was the strongest weapon he had to reserve against his relatives should they not do all he expected.

The shaken grandfather interviewed him in his study, where Malcolm Armit made the extraordinary proposal that he, Mr. Gillespie, should procure him the untenanted farm between the manse and Barnfingal where he and Lilith could live once they were married. Mr. Gillespie stared at him with his glazed eyes as though he could scarcely believe his ears, his blue lips twitched and his hand beat on the table before him. Procure him a farm? Procure him a farm? What was happening to everything? It had always been an ill-witched place, this Barnfingal, they should never have remained. He remembered his wife saying that years ago in the midst of an unprecedented storm of tears, that it was not fair to the girls and that Euphemia must go away for some months because she was falling into a decline. His wife's words had an uncanny way of coming back to Mr. Gillespie after she was dead with a significance they had never had for him when she had been alive. But they had remained at the manse, and now he was confronted by this clod of earth whom his only grandchild was forced to marry.

"Procure you a farm, young man? Procure you a farm, indeed? And where am I to get the money from to procure you a farm, I who find it quite difficult enough to keep a roof over my own head? You'll get no farm from me, nor would you if I had the Mint at my disposal. My grandchild has made up her mind to marry you for the sake of her child. That marriage must be kept as secret as possible, no one must be told about it. Are you understanding what I am saying? In the circumstances, which are most unhappy and for which you are entirely responsible, it must be as speedy as possible. You will travel as soon as you can leave your present employment to Darchester, near the Border."

"Ye'll need to gie me ma fare and keep."

"Your coach fare will be paid. Immediately you arrive at Darchester you will make arrangements to have the banns cried in the parish church. For my grandchild's sake I shall give you a letter which you will present to a relative of mine in Darchester. He will find as suitable work for you as he can. Otherwise you shall receive nothing out of this transaction. Care will be taken that everything is made out in my grandchild's name so that she may be able to live in a position approaching that to which she is accustomed."

"She'll be ma wife, whit's hers is mine—hoo she lives I live."

"I have no more to say. Go, now. I do not wish to see you again. And may God serve you as you serve her."

Walking back to Auchendee Callum had the feeling that he had permitted the old man to say too much and had himself said too little. But all that day he had not felt himself, for last night his sleep had been disturbed by a dream that had left an unreasonably lasting impression on his mind. He had dreamt Annie Lamont was pointing at him with her long finger, that all of her face was hidden in the shadow of her cavernous bonnet except a mouth which terrified him and which opened and shut to say, "'Behold, he travaileth with iniquity, and hath conceived mischief, and brought forth falsehood.'"

He left Auchendee within a week, and as he walked along the road by the Loch, his gaze on the ground, he knew that he would never again return to this country of bleak hills with their crude cairns and their paths stopping as abruptly as they had begun, with their crumbled sheilings and mounds like shallow dug graves. Springs would come with their sudden, misty showers and belated snow-wreaths, but he would not be there to see. The spated burns would charge down the hill-sides. The country would become saturated with the myriad colours of autumn. The leaves would be wrested from the trees, the air filled with the acrid scent of leaf mould. Long after the sun had disappeared, beams of light would be imprisoned in the mountain fastnesses. They would light up eerily the lochans and streaming burns, and drain the colour from the brightest trees.

Every step he took was bearing him farther from it for all time, and from the farm that stood on the hill, with its gaping door, ghostly crops and gIant stacks.

Chapter Six

NAPIER RAND told himself that the matter was closed now, finished, and accordingly tried to dismiss it from his mind as he would have a case which had failed in the courts, but he found to his dismay it was more difficult than that. By concentrating on his work, by willing himself with controlled determination not to think any more about it, he was able to believe that he had attained forgetfulness. But in spite of himself, when he thought he was thinking of quite other things, he would find he was in a deep reverie about her, his every movement arrested. Memories of her would come to his door like pale, frail beggars, seeking admittance. After all, he would ponder uneasily, a case was not finished until all the costs were paid; then he would tell himself quickly that the payment of Lilith Gillespie's debts had nothing to do with him. But had they not? He was her trustee; legally he was responsible for her. Again he would feel her small, cold hands over his, see again her drawn, white face, and wonder if he were not responsible for her morally as well. She had confided in him and he had not helped her, she had confessed to him and he had repelled her.

One evening, when his mother had gone to visit her sister and he was alone, he found it difficult to settle amongst his books and papers. The printed words conveyed no meaning to him and he read the same portions over and over again. He told himself that he was tired and sat with his opened book upside-down on his knee while he gazed thoughtfully into the fire, but he soon grew restless. He rose and crossed the room for his pipe, but he had no sooner reached the other side than he wondered what the devil he was looking for. His pipe, of course—he recollected it almost immediately and puffed it alight, but it did not soothe him as it usually did, its familiar smell brought him no comforting sense of tranquillity. He became irritated by his restlessness—he who prided himself on being the master and not the slave of his thoughts.

The other man would marry her, he stated suddenly to himself, as though determined to think the matter out once and for all. She had said so herself. If he would not, things might have been different. Of course she had said also that she did not love him; she had appealed, not to the other man, but to him to save her because he had loved her. Yes, yes, of course he had, but this discovery had made a difference, was bound to make a difference. He had loved her because to him she had been the embodiment of everything that was fair; but when one found one's loved one was not what one had imagined, one's love turned to stone. But did it? One had so little hold over one's emotions, they were not like orderly briefs or methodical affidavits but blew in all directions like pages in the wind.

He did not love her as he had loved her before, and yet—and yet he could not drown the memory of her beseeching eyes or forget that voice indrawn on sobs. He might at least have been kindlier, gentler. She was in pitiful trouble. He only realized now how terrible it must have been for her; he had been thinking so much of himself before. The horror of what she must have gone through, be going through, swept over him. He wondered tensely what she had done, if she had told her aunts …Then a thought struck him and it seemed to freeze his every nerve. But no, no, that could not have happened. It was over a month since he had been at the manse and he would have heard, he would be bound to hear …only he did wish he could blot from his mind the recollection of the grey Loch surrounded by those watching, graven mountains.

He realized suddenly and decisively that he could not forget her, no matter what she had done; nor could he, he found, despise her. God, who was he to condemn? She was only a child, eighteen or nineteen, he had forgotten which. He could not desert her; after all, he still loved her, he must still love her or he would not feel towards her as he did.

He determined he would leave to-morrow morning for Barnfingal. Then he made up his mind to leave that very night. He could not bear to remain inactive, he was seized by a feeling of urgency that nothing but speed could satisfy. Yes, he would leave that very night, even although by doing so he would have to spend two nights instead of one on the journey and only arrive a little earlier.

He would take her abroad, they could stay there perhaps a year and then return. And his mother? He paused in his hurried exit and drummed his fingers impatiently on the wall. Well, his mother must never know the truth. She would need to be told the position, for the marriage would have to take place as soon as possible, but he could say the child was his.

He told himself that once he was in the coach and well on the way he would feel different, but no coach could outstrip his galloping thoughts and stalking doubts. He tried to brush them from him, tried to reassure himself by considering how many premonitions never come to pass, but he was pursued by a feeling of foreboding. It strengthened as he proceeded on his journey. Everything went wrong until he wondered if some malignant fate were deliberately conspiring to keep him back. He lost his connections and twice the coaches he was in broke down. Anxiously he scanned the occupants of passing vehicles in case she might be driving away from Barnfingal as rapidly as he was driving towards it, and once his heart leapt when he saw a young face framed in a blue bonnet.

He arrived at Dormay at evening when the setting sun was shining on the gable ends of the cottages which formed the uneven village. At the inn he ordered a carriage to be harnessed instantly and chafed because they took so long. When he sat in it and was being driven to the manse he swore to himself that he could have walked quicker.

The sun had dropped behind the mountains and left the world gloomy and suddenly cold. He peered up at the rocks which towered above the road at one side and saw that small, old, ashen-grey trees, almost indistinguishable, grew on their dangerous sides. He found himself wondering whom she could possibly have met in this forsaken place ...

The old man responded to his summons at the door. Something, perhaps a fear of hearing what he dreaded to hear, restrained him from asking for Miss Lilith Gillespie. Instead he asked if he could see Miss Elizabeth; he had forgotten about the other sister, Euphemia.

He was shown into the living-room, where she lay on the couch, and something in her face confirmed his worst fears. They trooped upon him in all their hopelessness like dwarfs from an unblocked subterranean passage. For a long time he looked down at her, steeling himself, before he said,

"She has gone?"

"She left a week ago with Alice."

"Where did they go?"

"To Darchester."

"Darchester! Why did they go there?"

"That was where she was to be married."

His face twitched.

"Perhaps I would not be too late if I followed now?

He spoke carefully, quietly, as though afraid his very words would shatter so slender a chance.

"She was to be married to-day," said Elizabeth, her head bent.

Something seemed to break within him.

"And the man?" he managed to say at last. "You are sure he will be kind to her?"

He found her level grey eyes were raised to his.

"He is the last type of man she should have married. He trapped her. He is not even of her class."

"What do you mean by that?"

"I mean he was a carter at Auchendee."

He stared down at her, his face aghast, his bitter mouth twisted.

"Good God, and you allowed her to marry him," he said at last.

"She would not have the child born illegitimate."

Her ghost seemed to be haunting the deathly still manse, where the very ticking of the clock sounded subdued. He felt even if the place were razed to the ground her ghost would still remain. It followed him up the winding path to the gate, where the restive horses reared their heads. He told the driver he was in a hurry and, urging him to speed, leant back in the carriage and closed his eyes.

Chapter Seven

MR. GILLESPIE'S cousin in Darchester was a tea-merchant and, before he saw Callum, he thought of taking him as a clerk into his own office; but whenever he looked up from his desk and saw Malcolm Armit standing like a frowning rock before him, he realized the impossibility of this. The fellow did not look as though he knew even how to write, far less count. He found him instead the position of foreman in a weaving factory. Callum had been at work for more than a week when Lilith travelled down to Darchester with her Aunt Alice.

She wondered drearily if there had ever been so dismal a wedding. There were no epergnes and tea-sets, no silver-edged invitations, no fairy bridal-dress—none of the accompaniments to a wedding which in other circumstances she would have so delighted in. Only in the register was it duly recorded that on the thirtieth day of May, 18—, Lilith Ann Gillespie became the wife of Malcolm Armit, 'parentage unknown'.

Elizabeth had warned her sister what he was like, but Alice found him even worse than she had expected. He looked, she thought, just the kind of creature whose mother had hung him up when young on a thorn bush under the moon. His mother ... it was so difficult to grasp that his mother was her sister Euphemia. So he had grown up like this, that baby none of them had ever seen who had been left at Stonemerns years ago. As she looked at him with his too long arms and too long hair, squat nose and intent gaze, Alice was conscious of something strange about him. He had no intellect, of course, he looked even wandered at times, as though he were concentrating on nothing; but that was not what struck her so much as the impression he gave her of great strength allied to great weakness. Two forces were warring within him and the weakest would win.

She hated leaving Lilith with him, but Lilith's mind was so numbed she did not seem to be taking in what was going on around her. It was this stupefied apathy which wrung her aunt's heart, which made her kiss her over and over again as though in a vain attempt to reach her.

Passively Lilith would watch him bending over his food and find herself marvelling at the engrossed way he sat at table only for eating's sake. Very seldom they spoke to each other, never again did she give him the unguarded bursts of confidence she used to do in the Barnfingal days. Sometimes he would raise his eyes to find hers upon him and they would seem to say, "I know you now. I know you now. I know exactly what you are now." When she was alone the enforced dispassion would fall from her and the recollection of him would sweep over her in unutterable revulsions.

They were like two people from different planets compelled to live together. It irritated him when he saw her examine closely every cup and plate before she used it. "If ye're so parteekler aye looking for dirt, ye'll find it," he once informed her morosely. Her fastidiousness about even the tiniest details of dress mystified him; and he never grew accustomed to her bottles and jars and the little cambric bags in which she kept her hair-brushes.

Aunt Elizabeth wrote to her that Napier Rand had called again at the manse. When she read her words Lilith burst into a paroxysm of sobs so violent they seemed to tear her very heart, but she kissed the letter wildly and slept holding it in her hot hand until it became so creased it could scarcely be read.

In the merciful, longed-for dark she wept for the tall, fair splendour of Napier Rand. Her feverish thoughts dwelt on him with an unfluctuating constancy, drew comfort from the knowledge that he was somewhere in the world, aloof, inaccessible, but there. He was like a distant mountain, standing clear-cut and still against the sky, in a world where everything else was confusion, changing, chaos. To think of him was her only consolation, to see him again in her memory looking down at her with his keen, deep-set eyes. She knew she could never forget him, but she prayed that time would not dim her remembrance of him, that she would always be allowed to recall at will his every feature and glance.

Oh, if only, if only she had never met Malcolm Armit, how different everything would have been. She gazed at him with staring eyes and wondered how she had ever seen this troll she had married as anything but grimly ugly. Her mind faltered when she remembered how confidently she had put her hand in his in the days when he had told her that the right name for foxgloves was witches' thimmles and that knurs on trees were known as gipsy knots.

Ah, what black magic had he brewed in the poisonous foxglove, what irrevocable knot had he tied in her life, what spell had he weaved over her with his strange words, spoken in an unfamiliar dialect?

The child, a delicate little boy, was born one day at noon. Lilith, looking down at him through a haze of pain, could scarcely believe that he belonged to her, and he was so unlike her husband that no one would ever think he belonged to him. He was so fair skinned, so tiny, every detail about him so perfect. She wanted to weep over the minuteness of his finger nails. She loved to feel his little weight in her arms, to kiss the down on his head, to watch him, marvelling, as he lay so seriously asleep. Sometimes she would bend over him and gently push back the shawl from his puckered face to see if the mole, like a mistake, at the corner of one of his eyes was still there.

He meant so much to her that it was as though she felt by his birth she had been given a second chance. She liked to do everything for him herself, for she did not consider the midwife handled him with sufficient care. The good-natured, over-familiar woman would smile indulgently all over her large, broad face at the young mother's apprehensions. "It's no the first that's been born into this world," she would remark, "and," she would add, as though cautioning her not to depend on anything so inconsequential as a baby, "it's soo small by far." To which Lilith would reply almost fiercely that she had never wanted a big baby.

Callum thought it a poor-looking thing—just the kind of child she would have. It gave him no satisfaction to see it clasp and unclasp its hands, he considered it no miracle when it silently opened and shut its rounded mouth. His heart was not stabbed with pity when he saw its small, helpless body quiver just before it began to wail. He was of the opinion that, if it did not receive so much attention, it would cry a good deal less.

His hours at the weaving factory were long, but he missed the bodily, sleep-welcoming fatigue which his manual labour at Inchbuigh Farm and Auchendee had brought him. Also he did not mix well with other men. His employers had no reason to mistrust him for the output of work under him was increased, nevertheless he was disliked both by those over and those under him. The score of weavers he superintended were hostile. It was not so much that they resented a complete stranger being put over them as this particular stranger, with his alien personality. He was a foreigner to them, this dark, dour man, who made them work so hard, with his big head bent in deep thought as he walked silently through the weaving-rooms between the thrumming looms. Once or twice he wondered if he were going to escape after all from the evil thing that was pursuing him. If he helped to mend a broken loom and a thread snapped in his fingers, he was reminded forcibly of Mr. Cameron's denouncement. When he saw the men stop speaking amongst themselves as he drew near, he wondered if he were always to remain an outcast amongst his fellows, but he would pretend not to notice and would hastily tell himself, "If I bide lang enow it will pass. Juist ye bide a wee and they will come a' richt."

Chapter Eight

ONE night, in the heart of winter, he returned home later than was his custom, and, not finding his wife in the living-room, he went into the bedroom, where he saw her with the child in her arms. It was usually asleep in its cot by this time and it seemed to be sleeping now, for it made no sound or movement.

Callum sat down on a chair and watched them, but his wife was as oblivious of him as though he had been a table. Lately he had been conscious of a change in her attitude towards him. Sometimes her gaze fell upon him, as it was impossible for it not to do, but he realized that now she was simply not seeing him when she looked at him, as she never heard him when he came into a room. If his hair had gone white in a night she would not have noticed. This was the only resistance she could build up against him, and she had done it half unconsciously. Once he met her outside by chance and she had received such a shock at seeing him that her stricken face had whitened perceptibly. He felt as though he had forced himself back into her life after she had imagined he had become only a shadow.

She rose to her feet and began to pace restlessly about the room, humming almost inaudiby below her breath. She seemed taller now than she used to be, for she had grown much thinner. Every few minutes she whispered endearingly to the child in her arms as if to comfort it.

It was something in the baby's attitude, something in the bluish pallor of its face, that made Callum look at it with concentrated attention, but he did not speak for some time until she sat down again and began to rock it gently in her arms.

"There's no guid doing that," he said, "for it's deid."

She looked up wildly and glanced about the room to find where he was sitting.

"What's that?" she said loudly. "What's that you were saying?"

He did not answer, but sat watching her. She drew a long breath that rasped in her throat.

"Dead?" she said. "He can't be dead. His eyes are open."

"Some folk dee wi' their een ope."

She gazed blankly at him, every part of her tautened body mutely appealing to him to say it was not true. Slowly she looked from him to the weight in her arms, touched with one finger its waxen cheek. Then frantically she kissed its still face as though trying to warm it into life again; in an agony of love she held it to her as though striving to revivify its feeble heart with her own frenzied beats. She breathed on its hands, she chafed its stiffening feet, and her widened eyes almost imagined once or twice they saw movement flicker across that unseeing face.

She absorbed at last the knowledge that it was dead, although she did not stop rubbing its hands until long after the realization. She laid it in the bed and found herself tucking its clothes under its chin, for she had always had a morbid fear of its being suffocated. Then she turned, her hands to her face, and saw her husband sitting in a corner, leaning forward on his chair.

"You've killed him," she said brokenly, steadying herself by holding on to the bed, "it's your badness that's killed him. I might have known he wouldn't live, couldn't live, because of you." Something tightened in her throat and she could say no more.

Chapter Nine

HE never turned round quite quick enough. He never saw what was going on behind his back, was only conscious of being furtively watched, of looks exchanged as he passed, of half smiles and heads being nodded in his direction.

Was there something strange about him? Was he any different from other people? In his intensity to know he had once been able to get out of himself, to see himself dwindle down the long room as he walked the floor covered with the ends of warp and weft threads. Nothing had ever given him the horror of that, for he had seen himself as others would see him, and he seemed quite different to everyone else.

He walked through the weaving-rooms more than a score of times each day. Sometimes he never heard the noise of the looms. At other times it strangely excited him and wound him to such a pitch he was seized by a paralyzing fear, of its stopping. As one feels in certain dreams, he felt that if it ceased something would happen so appalling his brain could not conceive it. When the busy whir of one of the looms slowly lessened, like a top spinning its last, he would pray inarticulately for some tireless hand to speed it on and on and on, to feed the spindles with an inexhaustible supply of yarn. But one by one the thrumming of the looms would cease, leaving the air above them throbbing, and the weavers would see him standing there, his hands clenched behind his back, his shoulders drawn up, his eyes like coals, and they would complain to one another, "He would keep us at it if he could until our hands were bones."

One evening, at closing-up time, he went forward to the bench for his keys, but they moved beneath his fingers like live things and evaded his grasp. He grabbed at them and they slid along the bench. He waited a moment and then firmly picked them up by tightly holding the longest key. He lifted the bunch to his nose and smelt them. Yes, they had been soaped; someone had rubbed them in black soap.

If he turned round quickly now, in an instant, would he catch them? But no, he must not do that. They were watching him, waiting to see what he would do. He must pretend he had noticed nothing.

He was so determined not to hurry that he crossed the floor with marked slowness. None of them looked at him. One, his eyebrows raised and his mouth round, was whistling. Another was grinning behind his throstle frame. A third swore and sucked a damaged thumb.

So they had not been accidental, as he had tried to make himself believe, those small incidents that had happened to him at different times: finding his hat one day, his pockets another, filled with chaff and stour, his jacket sleeve torn from arm-hole to cuff as if ripped by a nail. That catgut stretched across his path had been to make him trip.

He walked home through the thronged, wet streets, conscious now, as if his body had grown suddenly sensitive, of being jostled and pushed and elbowed.

He opened the door and entered his home, then he paused in the dark hall and waited. Something had happened. He felt that at once; the house was emptier than when he had left it. As one knows when one is about to miss a step going downstairs, he knew he would find Lilith had gone.

He went into all the rooms, but she was in none of them. He did not call to her, for he knew the sound of his own voice would terrify him. There was a note lying on the red tablecloth in the living-room. He picked it up carefully, opened it and read :

I married you for the sake of our child. Now he is dead I can no longer remain with you. Nothing will ever make me return.
LILITH.

He sat down at the table and stared so hard at the cloth that his eyes seemed to dissect it, to see its warp threads unwound from bobbins, passed on to the beams, threaded through healds, criss-crossing the woof threads, webbing together ...

There was no escape. For him to strive to free himself was like a tree striving to escape from its roots deeply grafted in soils it had never seen. The Evil Eye pursuing him was his own.

Chapter Ten

HE saw it all so plainly now, as though it were laid out on a map before him. He thought he had been followed by unhappiness, dogged by calamity, but he had not; the unhappiness and calamity were coming from himself. Wherever he had gone he had brought disaster with him. Mr. Cameron, a minister of God, had known he was in the presence of evil, had adjured the assembled crofters and farmers and elders to beware, had warned them that it would contaminate and taint all those it came in touch with. He remembered Fiona lying at his side, calling out to him, "Wha throws the first trout oot will be marrit first. Hey, Callum Lamont!" She had thrown out a rat instead of a fish. That rat was symbolical of him, a foreboding to her of what was to come. Joe would still be alive if he had not listened to his unseen prompter. If it had not been for him crouched in the settle, moving about the outhouses of Inchbuigh Farm, herding the swaying cattle with their flicking tails to the hills, something would have happened to save Gilhead and Larch, they would never have been brought to so grievous a pass.

He felt if he plunged his head in Janet MacDiarmid's icy well, it would not cool his fevered brain. His thoughts could find no place to go. The world rolled away from him, leaving him the only speck of humanity on a bleak, deserted shore, conscious of but powerless before the inevitable incoming tide.

Wherever he went he carried his fetch (wraith of a living person) with him. He was one of those who were not chosen. People felt there was something strange about him, that was why no man would know him. That was why he was always outside closed doors and shuttered windows; he belonged only to haunted places where bats flew and owls screeched, to bare mountains where those long of tooth and claw dwelt.

Was it because he had not been born right, because he had come unwanted into the world? Were his mother and father to blame, or did the blame lie within himself? Again and again the question echoed through his brain.

He wanted to call out loudly, to challenge something; he was seized by an overpowering desire to communicate with someone, something, even the powers of darkness; but he did not speak, for he knew there was nothing to challenge, knew the hobgoblins would only throw back at him the shreds of his own voice.

He lifted his head slowly as though it were a great weight. Then, like a heavenly answer to his unspoken call, came the thought that perhaps he was possessed of this evil thing because he might not be baptized. Annie would know, Annie could tell him. He must find Annie, tell her of what had been working within him, speak to her until hours wheeled by, until his mouth dried and his breath whistled, even if she did not understand.

He sat there far into the night before he rose to start out on his journey. His brain felt like an empty house through which the wind rustled, shutting some doors, forcing open others.

Chapter Eleven

KNOWING there would be no coach at so late an hour, he began to walk northwards. He walked until the blackness lightened imperceptibly into dawn and until the things that loomed shapelessly through the greying dark formed into houses and trees. At an early hour in the morning he reached a large manufacturing city where the workers were streaming from the grimy streets to their factories and mills. He shrank from seeing them and being seen by them, so he went into a cart-shed, where he lay down on some sacks and slept. He had put nothing under his head, and he dreamt he had giant's shoulders and a pigmy's head which, owing to the bulk of his shoulders, could find no rest when he lay down.

A coach, bound for the north, left the marketplace at ten o'clock that morning. He entered it, determining to take it as far as it went and to walk the rest of the way to Stonemerns. He sat forward on his seat, looking neither to the left nor the right, never even raising his head. A terrible depression emanated from him, and the seats all round him were left empty. The guard thought he was ill and went forward to speak to him, but changed his mind and drew back.

He stayed that night at an inn, leaving it very early in the morning and beginning to walk once more. There were no factories now. The houses had given way to scattered cottages, the high buildings to lonely farmhouses, the cobbled streets to a rutted road. The snarling winds kept close to the low dykes that sometimes accompanied the road on its journey. He never rested but walked steadily on, until he began to taste salt on his lips and feel a biting tang in the wind. They brought back to him the memory of a squalid harbour and empty nets, the ever-craving, ever-crumbling sea, newly-scrubbed flags and the stench of curing fish.

He came upon a signpost at cross-roads, and recognized before him the road he had taken long ago to Inchbuigh Farm. He had stood, he remembered, underneath the signpost and wondered where the highway he was coming down now led to. He had been baffled as he thought of all the roads and pathways winding over the world which he could never take.

The track to Stonemerns forked from the high road and lay over the moors. Everything was quite familiar to him now. He saw the village huddling in the far distance. As he drew nearer it struck him as looking wasted, as though the sea had drained through all the cottages.

He passed the low schoolhouse and, half a mile farther on, the waste land with its piled dung heaps which was just outside the village. Once more he heard his feet echo in those narrow streets, where the little winds peaked and plained and pined.

Through an opened door came the sound of some women talking in their characteristic flat voices as though their monotony were in cadence with the distant sea. He met no one, although he was conscious after he had passed some of the cottages that their occupants came to their doors and looked after him to see whom he was.

Annie's was the last one of all. As he approached it he saw someone was kneeling in the doorway, evidently scrubbing the step, their boots protruding from draggled petticoats. He was surprised, for it was late afternoon, Annie had always had her step scrubbed the morning. But as he drew nearer he saw the boots were not Annie's, it was someone quite different from her who was washing her step. He had never seen this kneeling woman before. He stood beside her, and when his shadow fell over her she looked up, startled.

"Whaur's Annie Lamont?" he asked her.

"Annie Lamont?" she repeated stupidly.

"She bides in this hoose."

The woman's uncomprehending face cleared.

"Na, no noo," she corrected, "but I mind noo I heard them lift her name when I came here at first. Did ye no ken? Annie Lamont's deid."

She had risen to her feet and was unpinning her skirts at the back, letting them fall over her wet petticoats. The woman in the next cottage came to her door to see what was happening and, recognizing Callum, spoke to him.

"Ay, she de'ed on the twenty-fourth o' April o' this year," she said."We broke into her hoose that day syne she had no oped her door and would no answer oor chapping and ca'ing. We foond her deid in the kitchen bed. We took it in turns to keep her lyke-wake" (watch kept over a body between death and burial) "syne she had no folk o' her ain to do it for her, and they buried her aside her mither in the graveyard. It's Mistress Fisher wha bides in her hoose noo."

She waited, standing with her arms folded, as all the women stood in Stonemerns, expecting him to ask her questions and details, but he did not speak. She raised her voice as though under the impression he were deaf.

"Ye'll be tired wi' your journey," she said. "Ye can come ben and sit in ma kitchen for as lang as ye like."

But he shook his head, and they watched him walk along the path which led over coarse grass and intractable heath by the edge of ploughed fields to the sea.

He wanted to be alone as he had never wanted to be alone in his life before, he wanted to hide from searching, curious eyes, to go somewhere where he was sure he could not be overlooked. He picked his way between the fishing-nets spread to dry on the shingle, and stepped from boulder to boulder until he stood, looking out at the empty wastes above the heavy seas, on the rock where he used to stand.

The sky was grey with clouds like dolphins and seals passing across it. As far as his eye could see, sweeping into the pale primrose horizon, with boundless breaker upon breaker, stretched the restless sea. The tide was coming in, growling and sucking at the shore, swirling up at the rock on which he stood, licking his boots. A damaged fishing-boat had been drawn up on the shingle, and every few minutes a knocking sound was heard from it as the wind whacked a piece of loosely-hanging rope against its side.

He was old, he had always been old, he was as old as the first curse. No longer did he feel, as he used sometimes to feel, that he held up the pillars of the world. Strange to think those feelings of tense excitement he had as a boy, that breathless sense of imminence, of something tremendous about to happen, should all end in this. But perhaps this was the moment of his life they had foretold. By becoming part of this unrest, he might find rest.

He watched far out at sea a seventh wave advancing towards him. It rolled nearer and nearer, its raised surf lips towering, plunging, falling. He waited until he felt it dashing against the rock on which he stood. Then he waded out to sea.

Printed in the United States
210102BV00013B/78/P